the ocean

A NOVEL BY

Cecilia Araneda

Produced by:

FriesenPress

Suite 300 – 852 Fort Street
Victoria, BC, Canada V8W 1H8

www.friesenpress.com

Distributed to the trade by The Ingram Book Company

The support of the Manitoba Arts Council is acknowledged.

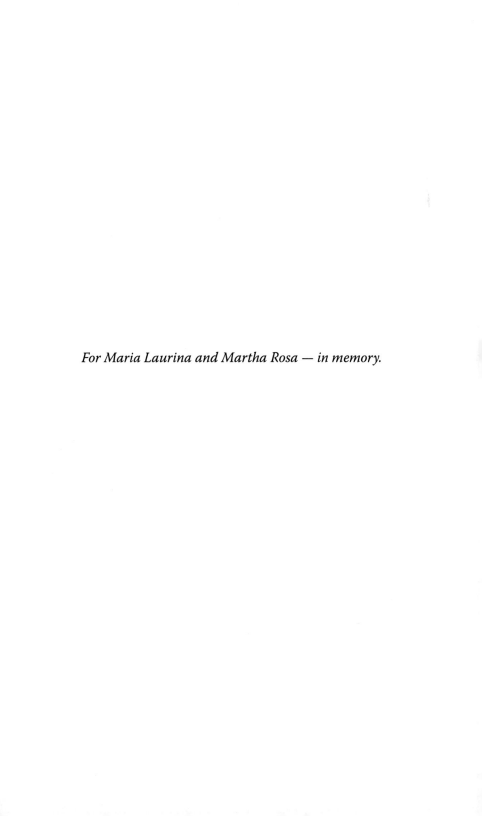

For Maria Laurina and Martha Rosa — in memory.

1.

The water soothed her, even though it was so very cold. It was much colder that day than it had ever been before. It instantly numbed her skin when she stepped in and she soon started to lose all sensation. She knew swimming in the ocean in the middle of the night was not a wise thing to do. The Gonzalez brothers had gone swimming after a night of drinking during the heat wave the summer before last and all three had disappeared, leaving only their sandals on the beach as testament. Their mother had tried to erect a shrine in their memory on the beach many times, but if it was not washed away by the water, it would be carried off by the wind, regardless of how strongly it was supported. Father Gutierrez was the only one who had been able to stop her from continuing to build it over and over again, convincing *Señora* Gonzalez that the sea itself was a natural shrine and that it was far grander than anything that could be built by human hands. The earth and everything in it, after all, were God's creation.

In that darkness, what Maria Soledad wanted was not to feel any more, and the night's ocean water gave her that. In it, she felt absolutely nothing.

Maria Soledad had always enjoyed swimming in the ocean. It took her away from all the fixed things that surrounded her on land. In it, she was not predefined: she was not a daughter and not a sister; and her chores could wait. Maria Soledad was the eldest daughter with nine brothers and it had become clear to her from very early on that being a girl was something that made her different. She had to help her mother in the house while her father and oldest brothers went off to work, but all her other brothers could do as they pleased to pass the day. Even into the evening, there were always dishes to wash and laundry that needed to be taken off the line and ironed. It was women's work, her mother would tell her, and she should be proud of that.

When she was younger, there was a time when Maria Soledad had not yet understood that being a girl made her different. Sunday afternoons, when her family would return from church and finish *almuerzo*, her father would take one of her brothers and teach him how to read using the bible. Maria Soledad had watched, fascinated, over many years as her father moved from one brother to the younger, knowing that her turn would soon come. When her father moved on to her younger brother, José, instead of her, she thought that her father had mixed up their ages and so she clarified to him that she was actually the elder of the two.

"Don't you think I know how old my children are?" her father Ramón asked.

"It's my turn to learn how to read, not his," Maria Soledad responded, not understanding why he hadn't realized that himself. "I'm older than him."

"You're serious, aren't you — ?"

And in that moment, Maria Soledad realized that he wasn't the one who had misunderstood.

"You need to learn the things that your mother teaches you and leave the reading to the boys," her father continued, patting her on her head, meaning to be endearing. "I'm sure your mother could use your help right now," he added after a moment, motioning for her to leave.

"Your father's right," her mother, Ana, tried to convince her later that evening when the two of them were alone in the kitchen. "There's a lot of pride in being able to take care of your family, and one day you'll have a family of your own to think of."

But Maria Soledad was so filled with anger by then that she refused even to look at her mother, let alone acknowledge in any way that she'd heard her.

"*Hija*..." Ana said after a moment, but Maria Soledad would not budge.

Instead, Maria looked out the kitchen door through the hallway and into the sitting room, watching her father and some of her brothers there, talking and laughing.

That summer, when Ana started to teach Maria Soledad how to knit and sew, Maria Soledad suddenly became all fingers. The sweaters she knitted were lopsided and would unravel easily, and the clothes that she darned would quickly made their way back to the mending pile again. Her mother patiently repeated her lessons once and twice again, thinking that perhaps all her daughter needed was a bit more time to understand. Ana finally did give up though, after persisting a few weeks longer without Maria Soledad showing even the slightest improvement.

"Isn't it odd that you would have so much trouble knitting and sewing when you've picked up everything else so quickly," her mother commented after excusing her from having to help with those tasks again.

Maria Soledad pretended not to have noticed the suspicion in her mother's tone as she got up from the kitchen table and left, not once stopping to look back.

Left without anything specific to do after *almuerzo* each day, Maria Soledad was able to go out and play for a while after clearing the table and finishing the dishes. Her mother had finally agreed to her going out alone, but only under the strictest of conditions that she return in time to help prepare supper, and so she was always careful to do just that. Those afternoons, Maria Soledad would go exploring in the fields just outside of town, where she'd found a fascinating world full of countless insects and butterflies. She would follow the butterflies, skipping and fluttering her arms along with them. She often wondered what it would be like to be one of them, as free as the air they floated on. Sometimes, she would catch a butterfly in her hands and then let it go, and as it fluttered up through the air again she could almost feel herself to be a part of it, if only for a brief moment.

Maria Soledad had just caught an especially beautiful yellow butterfly when she heard a soft voice from behind her.

"Can I have it?"

She turned to find a scrawny little boy standing a few feet behind her. He looked a few years younger than her, but what stood out the most about him was that he was so pale, with such light skin and hair and green eyes that were almost translucent. Maria Soledad had never seen anybody quite like him before — it seemed to her that somebody had taken a pencil eraser and half-erased him.

"Can I have the butterfly?" he asked again, unaware of how curious she found him to be.

Maria Soledad stared at him a little while longer and then let the butterfly go without responding to him. The boy was clearly disappointed but didn't say another word, though Maria Soledad had thought that he would. She looked at him a moment longer in silence, then finally continued on her way. The boy followed her from a distance, but didn't say anything more to her. Maria Soledad could see him trying to catch a few butterflies on his own here and there along the way, but he never moved quite at the right moment.

"Where did you come from?" Maria Soledad finally asked, unable to keep her curiosity to herself.

"I live down the road," the boy responded. "My name's Patrick Ross," he added after a moment.

"Patrick Ross — ?" Maria Soledad repeated, struck by how unusual it was. "That's a very odd name to have."

Patrick shrugged his shoulders in response. "Can you catch me a butterfly?" he asked again.

"Why do you want a butterfly?"

Patrick hesitated, her question seeming to have caught him unprepared. "Just to have," he finally responded after a moment.

"That's a silly reason," Maria Soledad declared before finally rushing off, not offering the boy any further explanation — she was concerned by the coming darkness and that she would be late getting home, but she did not feel the need to explain that to him.

"You what — ?" Ana asked her with an abrupt tone the likes of which Maria Soledad had never heard from her mother before. Her mother had asked her what she'd done that afternoon, and when Maria Soledad mentioned Patrick's name, that alone seemed to set Ana off. "Don't ever think of playing with him again — do you hear?"

"Why not?" Maria Soledad asked. She had not found anything especially interesting about the boy, except for the way he looked.

"Because your father and your brothers all work for the Ross family, and it isn't right for you to play with their son,"

Ana said. "And if you know what's good for you, you won't ever mention his name again — least of all to your father."

Maria Soledad nodded her head in acknowledgement, her mother's stern tone leaving no room for any uncertainty on her part, though it was the very thing that made her want to do the exact opposite of what she'd been instructed not to do. Yet, though Maria Soledad had thought that she'd put on her most serious of faces in responding to her mother, Ana did not let her go out again after *almuerzo* until many weeks had passed. When her mother finally did let her go back out, Maria Soledad could find no trace of the boy again, not that day or any of the days that followed. She finally decided that this was probably just as well, because he had bored her anyway — at least, that was what she tried to convince herself of.

Patrick did eventually reappear many weeks later, long after Maria Soledad had stopped thinking about him. This time, he carried a small, leather-bound book with him, and when he noticed Maria Soledad, he sat down and began to read it. Maria Soledad glanced over at Patrick a few times as she played, careful to keep her distance — not because this was what her mother had asked of her, but because she did not want to give him the satisfaction of knowing she was curious about him. Patrick did not look up from his book, though, not even once, and so Maria Soledad finally started to head back home.

"It's an English book that I'm reading," Patrick shouted from behind her, loud enough so there could be no way for her not to hear.

Maria Soledad stopped and looked back at him.

"In case you were wondering," he continued when he noticed that he'd caught her attention.

"I wasn't wondering," she told him, and that was the truth.

"Oh," he said, clearly disappointed with her response. "It's just that I thought you might want to learn how to read English."

"Why would you think that?"

"I don't know," he said, shrugging his shoulders, having lost all of his previous certainty.

"Don't you think that learning to read Spanish would be a lot more useful for me?" Maria Soledad asked, thinking that should have been obvious to him.

"You don't know how to read — ?" he asked back, clearly not having expected her response. "I can teach you that," he offered immediately as the idea formulated in his mind.

Maria Soledad hesitated for a moment. She did not want to say no to his offer, but she did not want to sound too eager either.

"I have a textbook at home that I can bring tomorrow," Patrick continued, correctly having interpreted her lack of response as a lack of refusal. "And then you can catch me a butterfly in exchange," he added.

"I'll catch you a butterfly *after* you teach me to read," Maria Soledad countered, certain there was no way for him to know just how much she wanted to learn how to read. "And, if you give me a book to keep," she added.

There were moments when Maria Soledad found herself saddened that she wasn't able to tell anybody that she was secretly learning to read in spite of her father's insistence that it wasn't for girls, but she did not ever dare mistake any moment of lightness on her mother's part to be an opportunity to share any honesty with her. She did, however, take comfort in the fact that she could feel herself learning and improving, and that once she was able to read, nobody would ever be able to take that away from her.

Finally, just as summer had started to come to an end and when Maria Soledad was reading words and sentences consistently and with ease, Patrick shut his textbook and held it out for her to take.

"This is yours now," he told her.

Maria Soledad eagerly took the book and started flipping the pages as though she were discovering it for the very first time. She felt each page as she came to it and let her fingers linger on the words that were imprinted on them, completely mesmerized by the idea that the book could actually be hers.

"You are going to catch me a butterfly now, aren't you?" Patrick asked, looking at her in a way that made her feel uneasy.

Patrick spent what seemed like an eternity to Maria Soledad picking out exactly the one butterfly he wanted, and Maria Soledad started to worry that if he took much longer she might not make it back home in time. Finally, he pointed to a bright, shiny yellow butterfly just like the one he'd seen her catch the very first time he'd met her. The butterfly fluttered through the air as though it were drunk, jerking suddenly in different directions, but Maria Soledad was able to catch it with ease.

"You're going to have to close your hands quickly over mine as I open them," she instructed Patrick, holding out her hands towards him.

Patrick was visibly nervous as he put his hands over hers, and Maria Soledad hesitated for a brief moment when she felt the warmth of them — for some reason, she had expected them to be cold. Finally, she opened her hands within his and then pulled them away quickly. Patrick suddenly smiled from ear to ear and she knew he could feel the butterfly's wings fluttering against the insides of his hands.

"You should let it go now," Maria Soledad said after a few seconds.

"What do you mean — ?" he asked, looking at her curiously.

"You need to let it go now. You can't keep it in your hands like that," she replied, thinking that should have been obvious to him.

"But you gave it to me."

"The butterfly's not mine. I gave it to you to hold," Maria Soledad clarified.

"You never said that before."

"What do you plan to do with it?" she asked, exasperated. "You're going to have to open your hands sooner or later."

"I'm going to put it in a jar, so that I can look at it whenever I want," Patrick replied.

"In a jar — ?" Maria Soledad was stunned by the suggestion. "It'll die in a jar."

"Not if I poke some air holes in the lid," Patrick responded.

"Let it go," she told him, not interested in trying to understand him any more.

Patrick looked at her, stunned by her tone.

"Let it go," she repeated again, this time in a far harsher tone.

Patrick finally ceded to her. When he opened up his hands, though, the butterfly just lay still in his one hand, its wings closed together. Maria Soledad stared at it, speechless — it had not occurred to her that the butterfly could actually die like that. Suddenly, though, the butterfly quickly stood up and flew away. But by then Maria Soledad had been filled with an immense feeling of dread that she could not shake. She stared at Patrick for a moment, and then suddenly ran away.

"Wait — ! You forgot your book," she heard him call out after her, but she did not stop.

"*Doña* Juana told me she saw you playing with one of the Ross boys outside of town the other day," Ana told Maria Soledad a few days later as Maria Soledad returned home to help with supper. By then, though, she had already stopped going out to meet up with Patrick.

"Why do you always have to do the exact opposite of what I ask?" Ana continued, frustrated. "It isn't always about you, Maria Soledad. When will you learn that?"

"I'm not going to play with him again," Maria Soledad told her mother, having sensed that it would be all right for her to say that — it was the truth, after all.

Maria Soledad did not return to the field outside of town again that summer, or any summer after. With her new ability to read, she found staying at home after *almuerzo* far more bearable. She would sneak out her father's bible when her mother wasn't looking and then excuse herself for a siesta, but secretly read instead. With her twin two-year-old sisters, Maria Lucinda and Maria Mercedes, napping in the bedroom with her, she knew she wouldn't have to worry about unexpected interruptions. Maria Soledad had had mixed feelings when her sisters were born, relieved that it wasn't yet another boy for her to look after, and yet feeling sorry for them at the same time. But at least then, when they were still such small and tiny girls, her twin sisters were able to sleep and dream without a worry.

In her father's bible, Maria Soledad found a world completely different from what she'd expected. There were far more stories within it than those that were read out on Sundays at church, and far more interesting ones, like the story of Jonah cast from his ship and saved in the belly of a whale. The places the bible spoke of seemed so expansive and vast, even magical. From her dark and tiny room, the only connection she felt to that world was in watching the ocean from her window — she knew the ocean water could reach all the way around the world and touch all of its shores, and she was certain that even there, so far away from everywhere else, it might carry a bit of every place in the world within it.

That one night many years later, the ocean called to her so strongly as she stared out at it from her bedroom window that she simply could not resist being within it. Her father had long ago put a stop to her swimming in the afternoons, telling her that she needed to help her mother more around the house, and so the quiet of night was all that had been left to her. As she floated in the cold ocean water that night, she let the waves wrap up around her and pull her as they wanted. The salt of the water should have burned her eyes and her mouth, but she was so numb from the cold by then that she could not feel anything other than her body swaying back and forth. Maybe, she thought, it could take her to another land that way, a world far away from that small town. Years before she was born, maybe even decades, a giant tsunami had come and washed away the town and it had to be rebuilt again by the survivors, and so Maria Soledad knew the ocean had great force and power and was capable of the unexpected. Suddenly, though, she felt the sandy ground beneath her and she realized that the ocean had pushed her back to the shore. She felt unsettled by that, and unsatisfied. There was nothing that she could command, no magic that she could conjure to take her away from that place.

2.

When supper was finished, Maria Soledad and her two sisters cleared off the table and started washing the dishes. From the kitchen, Maria Soledad could see her parents still seated at the dining room table even though everybody else had left. They were whispering to each other, clearly not wanting anybody to overhear what they were saying.

After a moment, Ana pushed back her chair and looked over to the kitchen doorway. "Maria Soledad," she called out, motioning her daughter over.

"Your father met a nice young man today," her mother continued as Maria Soledad walked into the dining room. "He's a police officer just commissioned in town. His name is Manuel Hernandez."

After Ana finished speaking, Maria Soledad continued to look at her, not understanding why she'd told her that.

"He's asked to take you out on a walk Sunday evening," Ana continued after a moment, anxiously glancing at Ramón beside her.

"Why?" Maria Soledad asked, still not understanding.

"So that you can meet a nice young man who's interested in meeting you," her mother replied.

"But why would I want to do that?"

"Don't talk back to your mother," her father quickly reproached her.

"But I'm not interested," Maria Soledad insisted, unaware of how insolent she was being.

Ramón stood up abruptly and struck her in the face.

"Ramón!" Ana pleaded with him.

Maria Soledad was caught off-guard by her father's reaction and looked at him as the burning pain of the impact of his hand against her cheek spread all over her face. She went to hit him back, an instinct beyond her conscious control, but Ramón quickly grabbed her wrist before she could reach him.

He was eerily calm as he held her arm. "You should think long and hard before you do something you *will* regret."

Maria Soledad looked at her mother then, but Ana would not look at her. She then noticed both her sisters staring at her from the kitchen doorway. When they saw her looking at them, they quickly retreated back into the kitchen, perhaps hoping that nobody else had noticed them. Maria Soledad turned back to her father then and stared right at him. She knew it was not a wise thing to do, but it was the only thing she felt able to do in that moment.

"This conversation is over and you *are* going out with Manuel," Ramón told her. "You misunderstood if you thought you had a say in the matter."

Maria Soledad watched her bruise grow over the next several days, fascinated by its progression of colours from blue and purple, to green, and then finally a faint yellow. When she looked at herself in the mirror, she was careful to look only at the bruise on her cheek and not her whole face. At some point, without knowing specifically when, she had changed profoundly and it disturbed her to see herself in the mirror. She was still not yet able to fully recognize the woman who stared back at her — it was a mix of her mother and her father, and even her two sisters, but only partially like any one individual person she knew.

She had just turned thirteen when she first began to suspect that something very strange was happening to her body. She had always grown out of her clothes quickly, passing down to the twins the things that had become too short or small for her, but then her clothes started to become tight around her hips and her chest, in a way they never had before. Even though a few years had since passed, she still wasn't comfortable with what had happened; people looked at her differently — expectantly.

Ana scurried around Maria Soledad in her bedroom that Sunday afternoon, making sure her daughter would be prepared for her planned walk with Manuel. Ana had picked out a dress for her and then pinned up her hair while Maria Soledad sat and watched. Partly, Maria Soledad was fascinated by the great effort her mother was expending and partly, she knew it was pointless to do anything else. Ana then pulled out some make-up from a box she'd brought with her into the room and tried to conceal the bruise on her daughter's face as best as she could.

"Cheer up. It won't be so bad," Ana tried to console her daughter. "Manuel has a very good job and you should consider yourself lucky that he's considering you for his wife."

Maria Soledad turned to look at her mother, stunned: "His wife — ?"

"Stop acting like such a little girl," her mother reproached her. "You need to find yourself a husband."

"But why is that so important?" Maria Soledad asked.

"I can't believe that you're actually asking me that," her mother replied. "Your father and I aren't getting any younger and if you don't find yourself a husband soon, God only knows what will become of you without any means of support."

When Maria Soledad finally met Manuel, she found him to be an exceedingly ordinary man. He was large and stout, and his movements were awkward and without grace. Their walk to the plaza that afternoon passed in almost complete silence, except for when he asked her if she wanted an ice cream cone. She said yes, hoping that it would at least provide her with something to help pass along the time.

"Thank you for the ice cream," she told Manuel later as he lingered by her front door after walking her home.

"Would you let me take you out again next weekend?" he managed to ask after an awkward silence had worked its way between them, seeming to have needed time to build up the courage to ask the question.

Maria Soledad hesitated, dreading the idea of having to spend even one more moment with him, but knowing that her parents were surely on the other side of the door and how they would expect her to respond.

Her date with Manuel the next week was virtually a carbon copy of their first, except that when they started to walk back home, they heard a car drive up behind them. Only the wealthiest families in town had cars and it was so rare to see one on the street that both Maria Soledad and Manuel turned back to have a look at it.

"Looks like the Rosses' new car," Manuel noted. "Their youngest son just returned from England and brought it back with him."

"Really?" Maria Soledad managed to articulate, suddenly growing very nervous.

Maria Soledad wasn't certain how long it had been since she had last seen Patrick. She hadn't seen him for the longest time after that summer he'd taught her to read, until one day several years later when she was accompanying her mother to the market. She noticed him in a coach that passed by on the street, headed out of town. He was dressed in a formal dark suit and seemed to be staring vacantly off to nowhere. He had changed from how she'd remembered him — his hair had darkened and his face had lost its roundness — and so it took her a moment to realize who it actually was. Patrick suddenly turned and looked at Maria Soledad as though he had felt her looking at him. He returned her stare with such a strong melancholy expression that Maria Soledad found it difficult to keep looking at him. She needed to look away and so turned to her mother beside her. By the time she dared to look back up again a few seconds later, the coach was further off down the road and all she could see of Patrick was his back.

As Patrick drove by her in the car now, it was obvious to Maria Soledad that he recognized her in the few moments it took him to drive by her and Manuel on the street. In a quick moment before he passed, their eyes met and Maria Soledad was left with the sensation that they were doing something illicit.

"It's a nice car, isn't it?" Manuel commented, perhaps thinking that was why she had stared at it for so long.

"Yes, it is," she answered after a brief moment, knowing that she had to say something back.

The twins rushed into their bedroom that afternoon after returning from the market and Maria Lucinda was careful to close the door quietly behind her.

"A woman who works for the Ross family stopped us in the market and asked us to give this to you," Maria Mercedes said, taking a small package wrapped in kraft paper from her bag and handing it to Maria Soledad.

Maria Soledad took the package hesitantly and just looked at it.

"I didn't know that you knew any of the Rosses," Maria Lucinda said.

"I don't," Maria Soledad responded, then noticed her sisters' look of disappointment. "It was a long time ago," she finally allowed after a moment. "A very long time ago."

"Aren't you going to open it?" Maria Lucinda asked.

"We were very careful not to be noticed," Maria Mercedes added, feeling the need to alleviate any concern Maria Soledad might have had.

"Very careful," Maria Lucinda concurred.

Maria Soledad looked at the package for a moment, then carefully started to unwrap it. Inside, she found the book that Patrick had used to teach her how to read, the book that he'd tried to give her that day. It instantly made her smile when she realized what it was, the memory having become lighter all those years later.

"A book?" Maria Mercedes asked, curious.

"Did she say anything when she gave it to you?" Maria Soledad asked.

"No," Maria Mercedes said. "Just that the package was for you."

Though the book and how it came to be passed along through them had left the twins with many unanswered questions, they eventually resigned themselves to accept Maria Soledad's cryptic explanations and finally headed off to the kitchen to drop off the groceries they'd bought.

Maria Soledad stared at the book in her hands for the longest time. She was surprised how the book made her feel, bringing back memories of Patrick that she'd long forgotten. And she was even more surprised that he'd given it to her after all those years.

When she finally dared open the book, she noticed a handwritten note on the inside cover: *"Please forgive me for having been young. How I wish I could see you again out in the field today."*

The note made Maria Soledad's heart start to pound hard, though she wondered if she'd understood it correctly. She wasn't even certain if the message was intended for her, or if it was, if it was intended for her on that day. She knew that it had been one of Patrick's old textbooks and so maybe the note had been there from before, a relic of other memories, though she couldn't remember having noticed it when she had been using the book to learn how to read. After inspecting the writing some more, Maria Soledad finally decided that the note was indeed freshly written and therefore must have been intended for her.

Without further hesitation, Maria Soledad quickly put on her shoes and headed out of her bedroom after checking to make sure nobody was around to see her leave. She made her way through town, very careful not to draw attention to herself by walking too fast, even though what she wanted to do was run. Only after she'd reached the outskirts of town did she dare rush any faster to make her way through the field, after she was certain that nobody could see her. Finally, she found Patrick in almost the very same spot where she'd left him almost fifteen years earlier, sitting under a tree reading a book.

"I wasn't sure you'd come," Patrick said when he noticed her, smiling, the way he looked at her making her feel nervous. "I wasn't certain if you'd even remembered me."

"It's been such a long time," Maria Soledad said, the only words she managed to find.

"My parents sent me to England to go to school."

"That sounds far away," Maria Soledad said, not certain she even knew where that was.

"It is," Patrick said. "It's almost on the exact opposite side of the world."

"Across the ocean?" she asked.

"Yes — across the ocean."

"I've never been even to Chillán."

"Do you have time to sit for a bit?" he asked after a moment.

Maria Soledad hesitated briefly, then took a seat beside him. She was no closer to him now than when they'd sat together as children that summer he'd taught her how to read, but this time it felt very different.

"Who was that man you were with yesterday?" Patrick asked.

"Manuel — ?" she asked. "He's a police officer my father knows."

"Are you two engaged?"

"Goodness, no," Maria Soledad was quick to clarify. "He's just somebody my parents want me to go out with."

"It's not what you want?" he asked.

Maria Soledad shrugged. The way in which Patrick had asked the question and the thickness of his tone made her feel suddenly self-conscious.

Before she could make sense of what was happening, she realized that Patrick was kissing her. After the moment had passed, Maria Soledad touched her lips — she needed to feel them, to feel again exactly what they had felt. She noticed Patrick staring at her then, and she did not know what to say.

"If I stay too long, my parents might find out that I'm gone," she finally said standing up, needing to take herself away from the heaviness that had come to surround her.

Patrick gave her a small smile and watched her leave without another word.

The butterflies were out in vast numbers that summer. When Maria Soledad walked through the field, hundreds of them would fly out from the grass, filling the air. The flutter of their wings in the sun looked almost like the ocean waves moving back and forth in a soft rhythm. Yet, Maria Soledad was too preoccupied to allow them to entrance her — all she could think of was Patrick. She replayed the moment they'd first kissed over and over again in her mind, the thought of it washing over her like a warm fluid. Even on the afternoons she would spend with Manuel, Maria Soledad could think of nothing else.

3.

After their first date, Maria Soledad continued seeing Manuel every Sunday afternoon. Her father was so pleased that she was being more agreeable that he eased up on some of the restrictions he'd placed on her and started to let her come and go as she pleased. In exchange for this freedom, Maria Soledad felt that seeing Manuel was something largely benign; indeed, Manuel asked for very little from her and seemed genuinely delighted in her presence alone.

With her parents no longer so concerned with how she spent her time, Maria Soledad was able to steal time away to be with Patrick. Often, they would meet at the storage shed on the Ross property, where they'd first made love. If Patrick was unable to meet Maria Soledad for some reason, he would leave a note out for her and she would linger over his words, for hours sometimes, retracing their forms with her fingers — she had never read anything as beautiful as the words Patrick used when he told her how much he loved her. It had never occurred to her that she could feel that way about somebody;

that she could want to be with somebody so much, that she would need to be with them.

"I still remember that day you left," Maria Soledad told him, after silence had comfortably wrapped itself around them.

"The day my parents sent me off to England?" Patrick asked.

"It seems like so long ago now."

"You wouldn't look at me," Patrick said. "You were still angry with me, weren't you?"

"No, I wasn't angry," she replied. "I think it was the exact opposite — I wished I could have looked at you, but I couldn't. I think I knew even then how much I wanted you."

Patrick moved in closer to hold her, wrapping his arms completely around her. Maria Soledad smiled then and allowed herself to enjoy the moment as it happened.

When Maria Soledad walked into the kitchen one evening before supper a few weeks later, the twins abruptly stopped talking and quickly rushed off to the dining room. Their sudden departure made Maria Soledad curious, wondering why they stopped their conversation mid-sentence when she walked in. Maria Soledad had been left with an uneasy feeling all day in the house, hearing whispers and catching quick glances in her direction, and the twins' actions now added to her sense that everybody was talking specifically about her. Even her brothers, who hardly ever paid any attention to her, suddenly couldn't stop looking at her either.

It was during supper though, when Maria Soledad noticed her father glance at her oddly, that her curiosity turned to dread and she suddenly grew terrified that this might all have to do with Patrick — perhaps somebody had seen them together or maybe the twins had told her father how often she went out at night. But then Ramón smiled at her when she served him supper, lifting her concern; if Ramón knew about her and Patrick, there was no way that he would not have already reacted by now. Regardless, not knowing what was *not* being said to her still left Maria Soledad with a deep sense of unease.

Manuel came by that evening a little earlier than usual to pick her up. They had been going out on walks together for several months now and he had grown more at ease around Maria Soledad over time. Today, though, he was just as nervous as he had been on their first date; all afternoon it seemed as if he wanted to say something to her, but every time Maria Soledad looked at him and gave him the opportunity to speak, he abruptly looked away. It was only after they finished their ice cream cones that Manuel finally spoke up.

"Will you give me the honour of becoming my wife?" he asked in a weak voice that suddenly gave all his nervousness away.

"Excuse me — ?"

At first, Maria Soledad was certain that she must have heard him incorrectly, but then he pulled out a ring from his pocket.

"I've already asked your father for permission to marry you, and he's given me his consent," Manuel told her.

Maria Soledad was completely stunned, both by Manuel and the way in which he stared at her waiting for her response — he held so much longing in his look, like a child wanting a piece of candy. She had no idea what to say to him or even what she could say, but before she could think of what to do next, an immense feeling of nausea came over her.

"Are you all right?" Manuel asked, noticing by her expression that she did not feel well.

She only managed a small nod in response before her legs gave out from under her and she collapsed.

Maria Soledad was not able to hold down any food for days after and stayed in bed, not finding the energy to do anything else — not even to go out to meet Patrick. She was concerned that Patrick might take her absence the wrong way and think that she wasn't interested in him any more, but then Maria Mercedes and Maria Lucinda snuck into the room one after-noon after Ana had stepped out for a bit.

"He stopped us on the street," Maria Mercedes told Maria Soledad.

"He wanted to know if you were all right. We told him that you were sick but that we thought you would be all right," Maria Lucinda added.

"Did anybody see you?" Maria Soledad asked.

"No," Maria Mercedes assured her. "We are very careful."

"You should rest now," Maria Lucinda added.

And with that, the two girls were gone.

Maria Soledad wondered about her sisters. They always seemed so much more certain about themselves than she had ever felt herself, even though they were so much younger than her. She had never once told them about Patrick, nor had they ever asked, and yet they did not doubt what they knew. Perhaps it was the two-ness of them, Maria Soledad thought.

Maria Soledad had thought nothing more about her illness over the days that passed until her mother came into her bedroom one afternoon and asked the twins to leave. Ana seemed preoccupied, as though something weighed heavy on her mind.

"You and Manuel haven't been doing anything that you should be telling me about, have you?" her mother asked after a moment, after waiting to be sure that the twins were beyond where they could hear.

"Like what?" Maria Soledad asked.

"I don't know. That's why I'm asking," Ana responded. "You haven't been this sick since you were a little girl."

Maria Soledad found her mother's posturing to be odd. It was not at all like her to be so vague.

"You and Manuel have been seeing each other for some time now. Sometimes a man will expect certain things from woman," Ana continued.

Maria Soledad assessed her mother's expression in that moment, wondering if she'd understood her correctly.

"Has Manuel asked you to do anything?" her mother finally asked directly.

Maria Soledad quickly shook her head in response.

"Are you sure?"

"Yes, I'm sure," Maria Soledad said, knowing that only a certain tone and absolutely no hesitation on her part would turn her mother from her train of thought.

"Well, maybe you do just have the flu after all," Ana said after moment, seeming resigned to her daughter's assurance, but not convinced.

Maria Soledad examined her naked body that night in the bathroom. She had felt so sick so suddenly that it simply hadn't occurred to her that she might be pregnant. It wasn't the first time that her period was late and so that in itself hadn't caused her any concern. Now, Maria Soledad was uncertain what to think — she did not know whether to be happy or sad, or if there was something else that she should feel.

"You're pregnant?" Patrick was visibly stunned when Maria Soledad told him, the vagueness of his reaction making her instantly worried.

"I can't believe this," he continued, suddenly smiling, instantly taking away all her worry. "This is better than anything I could have imagined."

"I don't know what I'm going to do," she confided in him.

"Well, I do," he said, taking her hands. "You'll just have to marry me."

"What?"

"We can leave before anybody finds out."

"What about our families?" Maria Soledad asked.

"This is our family now," Patrick said, touching Maria Soledad on her belly.

Early the next morning, Maria Soledad quickly packed the few things she felt she would need. Patrick had given her specific instructions to meet him that night, ready to go. After she'd packed her things, the only thing left for her was to watch the minutes go by on the clock until the entire day finally passed. By the time dusk arrived, she was so visibly restless that her sisters asked her if she was feeling unwell again.

When Maria Soledad finally went out to the shed after night had fallen, she found that Patrick was not there yet. She looked out towards the Ross house hoping to catch a glimpse of him on his way, but she saw nobody coming. After another while passed, Maria Soledad started to pace back and forth, unable to sit any longer. Normally, if something was going to keep Patrick, he would leave her a note — but this time Maria Soledad did not find one. She found it unbearable to have to wait for him even one moment longer, but knew there was nothing else she could do even as she felt hours pass, and so she forced herself to sit still and be patient.

Maria Soledad woke, startled, just at the break of dawn. She was confused at first, uncertain where she was, but then realized she must have fallen asleep waiting for Patrick and that he had not come. She wanted to wait longer, certain that he would still come like he said he would, but knew that if she didn't go home soon her parents would wake to find her gone. Everything was far less certain to her now and Maria Soledad was scared to think what Ramón would do to her if he ever found out about Patrick. Waiting any longer was too much of a risk for her, and so returning home as quickly as possible was the only option she had.

Maria Soledad returned to the shed that second night, certain that Patrick would surely be there waiting for her or at least have left her a note, but she found neither when she arrived. She waited for Patrick again into the night, but this time was careful to leave before her need to sleep consumed her. Maria Soledad felt herself drowning in loneliness as she walked home alone in the darkness that night, and this sensation made every step she took difficult. She felt in her heart that Patrick would never abandon her, and yet doubt still flooded through her mind.

After *almuerzo* on the third day, Maria Soledad changed into her best dress and told Ana she was going to the police station to see Manuel, but went to the Ross house instead. Though just the thought of going near the Ross house made her very nervous, she needed to know what had happened to Patrick and so she'd decided that walking up to the front door and simply asking was the only way she would know for sure.

"I'd like to speak with Mr. Patrick Ross, please," she asked when the maid opened the door, still nervous but knowing that giving that away would be of no benefit to her.

The maid was visibly stunned to see Maria Soledad and quickly stepped outside, shutting the door behind her so that the two could not be heard from inside.

"You stupid little girl! Don't you know better than coming around here?"

Maria Soledad was caught off-guard by the maid's words. "I know that Patrick will see me," she insisted.

"That's not for him to decide. His parents are the ones with authority around here and — *trust me* — they are not happy with him. They've already shipped him off to Santiago," the maid told her.

"Santiago — ?"

The maid gave Maria Soledad a harsh look of disapproval. "You're lucky he refused to give them your name. Your father and brothers all work for the Rosses and they can destroy your family. If you know what's good for you, you will walk away from here right now and never look back."

Maria Soledad stared at the woman, stunned speechless as she absorbed her words. After a moment, she bolted off, terrified. She ran all the way down to the beach, not stopping even for a second, not even as her legs started to burn, not even to catch her breath. It was only when she reached the sand where the waves crashed up to the shore that she finally stopped — she crumpled down to the ground and curled herself into a tiny ball. She cried and cried then, until nothing was left within her: no love and no hate, not even the slightest sensation of feeling. Not feeling, was the only thing that was able to soothe her.

That evening, Maria Soledad heated up water for a bath as she cleared the supper dishes from the dining room table. Every time the water boiled, she would go to the bathroom and pour it into the tub. It took several trips back and forth, but when the tub was finally full, she was able to close herself off entirely from the world around her, even if only for that little while.

Maria Soledad sat on the edge of the tub and swirled the hot water with her fingers, the motion of the water engrossing her. When she would change the direction of her hand, the water would soon follow — it was the only thing she could command.

When she finally got into the water, Maria Soledad immersed herself completely within it. Everything disappeared then: her mother and father, and even Patrick and the baby growing inside her. All that remained were the memories she had of when she was a little girl, running through the fields, chasing butterflies — she was as free as the wind that had swirled around her then.

As Maria Soledad emerged from under the water to take a breath, she noticed her father's shaving knife reflecting the light of the setting sun that streamed in through the small window. She picked up the knife and ran her fingers lightly along the blade of it, curious to feel how sharp it was. She accidentally pricked one of her fingers in doing that and instantly recoiled from the stinging pain, even though she had been certain it would be impossible for her to feel anything ever again. The blood from the cut rushed down her finger to her arm, and found a quick path to the water she sat in. She watched, fascinated, as the water quickly dissolved the blood and eliminated all traces of it. The water itself remained unstained.

"Maria Soledad," Ana called out from behind the door. "Hurry up and get dressed. Manuel's here to see you."

Maria Soledad stared at the closed bathroom door without moving or making a sound. She hoped her mother would simply go away if she offered no response.

"Are you listening to me?" her mother asked after a moment, her curt tone clearly showing her frustration with her daughter.

"I'll be right out," Maria Soledad finally replied, deciding it best not to test her mother any more.

Maria Soledad got out of the bathtub and pulled on her clothes as quickly as she could. She then opened the bathroom door to find her mother waiting for her right outside it with a frown on her face.

"I thought you went to see Manuel this afternoon," Ana said.

Maria Soledad did not know how to respond to her mother, given that Ana clearly knew she had not done that.

"Never mind," her mother continued before even giving Maria Soledad the opportunity to respond. "Manuel's come by for your response to his proposal, and you know what your answer should be."

"Yes, I do," Maria Soledad replied without even the slightest hesitation. She knew it was the only thing that remained for her.

"I hope you're feeling better," Manuel said as Maria Soledad walked into the front hall where he sat waiting for her.

Maria Soledad nodded in response, giving him a small smile.

"I thought if you were up to it, you could give me a response to my proposal," he continued, his words coming across as very well-rehearsed, with only a slight nervousness in his tone.

"Yes, Manuel, I will marry you," Maria Soledad replied automatically.

Manuel was visibly excited with her response. He quickly pulled out the engagement ring from his pocket and placed it on her finger. Her finger still stung from the cut, but it had stopped bleeding by then and there was nothing left to show what remained of her pain.

"I want for us to get married as soon as possible," she told Manuel.

"Of course. However you want."

4.

It was the ocean that Maria Soledad missed the most, and she hadn't expected that. Manuel's house was on the other side of town, away from the ocean, and when Maria Soledad moved in after their wedding she found the silence uncomfortable — she hadn't realized before just how much she relied on the faint sound of the ocean to lull her to sleep. Some rare nights in Manuel's house if she closed her eyes and concentrated, she could faintly hear the sound of the ocean waves crashing onto the shore off in the distance and she would be lulled to sleep that way. Mainly, though, the ocean was absent and Maria Soledad was left with the sensation of being oddly separated.

In the days leading up to her wedding, Maria Soledad had already started to feel herself being pulled away from her life. One morning, her mother told her brothers to lay out some trunks in her bedroom and instructed Maria Soledad to pack her things. Maria Soledad stared at the trunks for a while without moving at all. It had not occurred to her before that she would have to pack up her things and move out, although it seemed obvious to her in that moment. She hadn't thought about leaving her bedroom or the twins who shared it with her, or even the house she'd lived in all her life. Leaving seemed too simple; in Maria Soledad's mind, it should have been harder, and the vast separation between what was and what should be unsettled her.

"Stop dallying about," Ana told her. "You have a lot of packing to do."

When she finally started to fold up her things, Maria Soledad noticed that one of the trunks was already half full with the linens she was to take to her matrimonial home. Her mother had made them for her years earlier, when it had become apparent to her that Maria Soledad would not make them for herself, let alone sew or knit anything else. Maria Soledad fingered through the linens and was caught by how fresh and crisp they were. They were all neatly embroidered with matching floral patterns and she knew that she should like them, but their newness bothered her.

Maria Soledad added her own old sheets to the stack then, but Ana quickly pulled them back out.

"You can't take those old things to your new house," she reproached her daughter. "What would Manuel think?"

Maria Soledad found the notion that Manuel would think anything at all of what she did with her things to be curious, but she knew that her mother didn't actually want an answer to her question.

After she finished packing the last of her things, Maria Soledad surveyed what was left of the room. It felt very different with nothing of hers left within it — there was nothing that said she'd lived there all her life, not even the slightest sensation of all those twenty-four years. It had released her memory so easily from within it and Maria Soledad was more saddened by that than she realized she would be.

Manuel waited for Maria Soledad at the alter and at his side was another police officer, a man she had never met before. As Maria Soledad walked down the aisle holding her father's arm, she found it difficult to keep up to him because her wedding dress was far too tight. Her mother was married in that same dress almost thirty years earlier, when the lace had not yet yellowed with age. As an adult, Maria Soledad had grown up to be almost the exact same size as her mother, and given the quickness of her wedding plans, using her mother's dress was the only option she'd had. The first time she'd tried it on, though, she was unable to button it up fully.

"Isn't it odd that such a good fabric would shrink with age," Ana had commented then.

Maria Soledad had only nodded in response, careful not to make eye contact with her mother.

It was only after her mother had let out all the seams that Maria Soledad was able to fit into the dress, but only by tucking in her stomach. Walking down the church aisle now with her father, she found it increasingly difficult to breathe and soon found the tightness of the dress unbearable. When she reached Manuel, he took hold of her hand and the clamminess of his hand against hers only served to add to her discomfort. She tried to pull her hand away from his then, lightly tugging at it, but Manuel did not let go. Instead, he turned to her and smiled.

In church on Sundays, Maria Soledad always found Father Gutierrez's tone to be harsh and stern, and it was difficult for her to pay attention to him for any length of time. But today at her wedding she stood far too close to him for her to dare allow even the smallest lapse of attention. He did let the two of them kneel at the altar partway through the ceremony, however, and she was grateful for at least that.

"Eat of this bread and drink of this wine. It is the body and blood of Christ our Saviour."

Father Gutierrez placed the Eucharist in Maria Soledad's mouth and held out the wine goblet for her to sip from. The wine quickly dissolved the wafer and left a lingering sour taste in her mouth.

The morning of her wedding, Maria Lucinda and Maria Mercedes went to Manuel's house to unpack their sister's things and to get the house in order. Maria Soledad felt comfortable leaving her things in the care of her sisters, knowing that they would leave the smallest of the trunks unpacked and unopened — in that trunk, Maria Soledad had secretly stashed away all the books she'd amassed over the years. She would skim away part of the grocery money whenever she felt her mother wouldn't notice and save it up until she had enough money to buy a new book. She'd used those same books to teach the twins how to read, and so she knew that her sisters would be careful to keep them out of sight.

As Maria Soledad walked into the house that evening after her wedding, she instantly recognized the faint smell of lemons in the air that gave away to her that her sisters had been there.

"Don't you find it hot in here?" Manuel asked, walking into the house right after her. He opened the window and the evening breeze that came through it quickly dissipated the smell.

Maria Soledad followed Manuel into the bedroom and started to undress, assuming that was what he wanted by going into the bedroom in the first place. Manuel was hanging up his suit jacket in the wardrobe, and when he turned around and found Maria Soledad partly naked he looked stunned. Maria Soledad waited for him to say or do something, but he backed away instead and quickly left the room. Maria Soledad sat on the bed and waited for him to return, certain that he would — but he didn't, not even after a long while had passed. Finally, she decided to change into her nightgown and go to bed, not knowing what more she could do.

The loose fit of the nightgown finally let her breathe with ease and she was able to relax for the first time that day. When she turned off the light, though, she could hear what she thought was Manuel crying in the other room — the sound was faint but audible in the stillness that accompanied the dark. She wondered briefly if she should do something, perhaps go to him, but was unsure.

"I'll get that," Maria Mercedes said, getting up from the table when the water in the kettle started to boil. Maria Lucinda followed her twin sister into the kitchen and Maria Soledad could hear them moving about together, keenly preparing the tea.

The twins had fluttered in that afternoon unannounced, excited to see their sister the new bride. They treated her as though she were somehow more important now, even though Maria Soledad did not feel herself to be. The twins arrived dressed in their best clothes and brought with them an array of pastries fresh from the pastry shop, insisting they treat their sister to proper tea. The twins' insistence on having formal afternoon tea made Maria Soledad feel awkward at first, because she was neither prepared nor dressed for the occasion, but she was happy for the company nonetheless. Manuel had spoken to her very little since their wedding, and though that hadn't surprised her, she hadn't realized how lonely a quiet house could be.

"You have to tell us everything," Maria Mercedes said eagerly as she poured the tea, the twins giggling to each other right after, and Maria Soledad found it difficult not to smile.

Her sisters' curiosity about her wedding night seemed so innocent to Maria Soledad that she felt obliged to tell them a tale that would not destroy their lightness. She thought of Patrick again that afternoon — her memory of him had become strangely detached, as if he were somebody she'd read about in a book and not actually a real person who had been a part of her life. She thought it odd that somebody she'd once needed so desperately could fade so quickly from her memory.

Manuel arrived earlier than usual that evening from work and when the twins noticed him, they couldn't help but giggle. Their reaction made Manuel visibly uneasy and he quietly walked off further down the hallway. With Manuel in the house, the lightness that had surrounded that afternoon disappeared and Maria Soledad grew distracted wondering what he was doing. It didn't take her sisters long to realize that she'd lost interest in the conversation, though, and they soon left in the same flurry with which they'd arrived. It was only when Maria Soledad saw the twins out to the front door that she realized how dark the day had become. She watched her sisters as they walked down the street together holding hands and desperately longed to go with them. She was envious of their sameness, in the way that each had the company of herself in another person. She wondered if it was even possible for them to understand what it felt like to be alone and lonely.

After the twins disappeared into the growing darkness, Maria Soledad stepped back into the house and bolted the door shut. When she walked back down the hallway to the kitchen, she saw the light on in the bedroom and was caught by the stark shadows Manuel made as he moved around — something about them made her feel uneasy. The last few nights, Manuel and Maria Soledad had eaten supper together in absolute silence, the only sound that of the cutlery clinking against the plates. Tonight, though, Maria Soledad set up supper for Manuel alone in the dining room, deciding that she would eat in the kitchen instead. She thought this would make her feel more comfortable, as she would no longer have to dread the anticipation of conversation between the two of them. Only after she heard Manuel leave the dining room after finishing his meal did she venture back in to clear off the table and continue with her chores.

When Maria Soledad walked into the bedroom to retire for the night, she found her book trunk smashed open and her books strewn across the floor with ripped pages everywhere. Manuel was sitting on the bed with his head in his hands, and Maria Soledad would have thought him to be in pain if it weren't for the strong smell of liquor coming from him.

"What have you done?" she asked, horrified, crouching down around her books and sifting through them to assess the damage.

From the corner of her eye, Maria Soledad could see Manuel stand up. He walked over to her, but she didn't even have the chance to look up before he hit her, making her fall back into the trunk behind her. She lay still for a moment, not certain what had just happened, then looked up at Manuel, confused.

"How dare you mock me like that!" Manuel yelled out suddenly.

Maria Soledad could hear his voice, but the words were drowned out by the ringing in her ears. She slowly, carefully touched her face where he had struck her — her cool hand against her skin soothing the burning sensation she felt. After a moment, she managed to pull herself up without responding to Manuel, not knowing what it was he wanted her to say. Her lack of response only seemed to heighten his rage, though, because he struck her again, this time shoving her back up against the wall. Maria Soledad could feel a sharp pain radiating from her back up to her neck and her head as she hit the wall behind her. She looked at Manuel in that moment, her eyes tearing, the image of him blurred.

"How dare you insult me like that to your sisters!" he yelled out, this time even more enraged than before.

Manuel hit her again without giving her even a moment to respond. When she felt his hand strike her face, Maria Soledad wondered what satisfaction he received from that. She fell down to the floor this time, though she did not feel herself fall; instead, the floor rushed up to hit her face. Lying down on the ground, Maria Soledad suddenly felt a cool draft in the room. She hadn't noticed it before, but it animated the pages of her books and made them swirl along the floor. From where she lay, she could hear Manuel still screaming at her, but everything he said was washed out by the air moving around her and the pages it carried. The air was soft as it moved across her body and she found its coolness immensely refreshing, almost like the ocean water, its thick texture quickly moving in to envelop her and to give her comfort. Maria Soledad tried to taste the air then, curious if it was salty. Even with what happened next in the dryness of the world around her, as Manuel got on top of her, Maria Soledad remained focused only on that cool sensation, until she could feel no more.

When Maria Soledad woke, she could hear Manuel crying but did not look to see where he was — she did not care to know. She pulled herself up from the pages on the floor, her head throbbing and her body desperately sore. She carefully started to pick up the pages around her and smoothed them out one by one as best she could. When she realized the pages in her hands were from the book that Patrick had given her, she felt an immense desire to cry, but she did not allow herself that, refusing to give Manuel the satisfaction. Instead, she got up and started to head out of the room.

"Maria Soledad," Manuel called to her in a tone far more tender than she'd ever come from him before.

She turned back and followed his voice to find him curled up on the floor at the far corner of the room. He seemed small to her then, far smaller than she'd thought him to be before, more like a scrawny little boy than a man. His eyes pleaded with her, clearly seeking comfort and forgiveness, but Maria Soledad instead turned and walked away, continuing down the hallway without giving him another thought.

When she reached the bathroom, Maria Soledad was careful to lock the door behind her. She softly sponged her bloodied and bruised body, hoping the baby inside her was still alive. She thought that if there was any grace in the world, her child would be born healthy and able to survive. If she could give her child every last bit of strength she had within her, she would, but Maria Soledad did not know if even that would be enough.

5.

Maria Soledad took the washcloth and dipped it into the water basin. The water was cool against her skin and she allowed herself to enjoy it before wringing out the cloth. She washed her daughter carefully and softly with the wet cloth, cleaning away the blood from which she was born. She caressed her daughter's fragile body as it lay against hers, feeling her tiny heart pumping, its rhythm separate from her own.

Maria Soledad had lived with Manuel for not even a year yet, but they had come to an unspoken agreement: he did not require her to talk to him, and she gave him the courtesy of responding to his infrequent questions. On the odd occasion when Manuel would invite a guest home, she knew without words what was expected from her — theirs was not a personal relationship, they were simply husband and wife.

"Would you like another cup of tea?" she'd asked Father Gutierrez only a few weeks earlier.

"Yes. Thank you, my dear," he replied, holding out his cup.

Manuel had been visibly uneasy when the Father had come over unannounced that Sunday afternoon, perhaps trying to catch the two of them in their dishonesty.

"I must admit, it's rather a treat to see a young wife who understands her duties to her husband, especially this day and age when it seems that women are more interested in emotional frivolities than in tending to their duties," Father Gutierrez continued.

Maria Soledad gave him a small smile and quickly finished pouring the tea without a word, then started to leave the room.

"It's obvious you've worked very hard to make a good home here," she heard the Father say to Manuel. "Your new child will be very lucky."

Maria Soledad stopped when she reached the door and looked at Manuel as he listened to Father Gutierrez speak. Manuel caught her look with a brief, longing glance, seeming to have lost himself in the moment and forgetting all that could not be undone. After a moment, he turned back to look at the Father again, leaving Maria Soledad with an unsettled feeling.

The night Consuelo was born, the house was filled with Maria Soledad's screams. The searing heat of summer compounded the agony she felt in giving birth, and yelling helped her endure the pain. She had not once thought of Manuel or what he would have been thinking when he heard all the commotion, but when she turned to her mother to take her newborn baby, she noticed him peering in through the doorway from the hall and suddenly felt sorry for him. She motioned for him to come into the room, but he seemed embarrassed to have been discovered and instead quickly retreated beyond where she could see. It occurred to Maria Soledad only in that moment how much Manuel's own life had changed beyond his control, and how that would continue. But even though she'd come to understand him and even feel for him, there was much that remained between them that would continue to separate them.

"She's so beautiful," Maria Mercedes said.

"She looks just like you," Maria Lucinda added, but then said nothing more — almost abruptly so.

During the weeks after her daughter's birth, Ana and the twins were constantly in and out of the house, helping Maria Soledad with all her new chores. Maria Lucinda and Maria Mercedes, especially, made their sister's house almost their second home, flying in at the earliest hours of the morning and staying well into the evening, making sure that everything was completely spotless and in its place before leaving for the night. Maria Soledad was grateful for the help, but the presence of so many women put Manuel visibly on edge and that, in turn, made Maria Soledad nervous. Manuel moved around the house like a ghost, preferring to stay within the shadows of the house and unseen, reappearing only after the twins had finally left.

As Maria Soledad took on her new responsibilities, Ana and the twins started to come around less frequently and Manuel soon returned to his old routines. Consuelo's presence in the house no longer seemed to disturb him and Maria Soledad felt he was growing accustomed to her being around. Maria Soledad did catch him stealing glances at her daughter every now and then, but it seemed more out of curiosity than anything else, finding nothing disturbing at all in those looks.

Fall had arrived when Manuel came from work early one day as Maria Soledad was breastfeeding. She hadn't heard him enter the house and was startled to find him suddenly standing at her bedroom doorway, staring at her. She quickly covered herself up and looked straight at him, purposefully meeting his eyes to assess his intentions. Manuel appeared to be somewhere deep within himself, though, and either did not notice her looking at him or simply chose not to acknowledge that. Finally, after a long moment of silence had passed, he turned and walked off as quietly as he had come.

Maria Soledad found Manuel in his study later that evening, staring out the window lost in thought again. She stood in the doorway, unsure what to do — she wanted him to know that she was there waiting for him but didn't dare disturb him. She finally decided to knock lightly on the door, but he still did not acknowledge her.

"Do you want your supper now?" Maria Soledad finally asked in a soft tone.

When Manuel still did not respond even to her question, she decided it best to simply leave him to his thoughts and not bother him any more.

Maria Soledad prepared supper and set the table just like she did every other day, and then sat in the kitchen with her daughter close to her. She waited to see if she could hear Manuel go into the dining room, but he never did, not even as evening turned into night. Maria Soledad cleaned up the table hours later and then returned to the kitchen, gently rocking her daughter to sleep there. The day had exhausted her and Consuelo soon grew heavy in her arms, but she would have to pass by Manuel's study to reach her own bedroom and she did not want to risk doing that, not in the mood he was in.

Maria Soledad woke in the middle of the night confused and startled, uncertain where she was or how long she'd been asleep. She had lain down with Consuelo on the kitchen floor after her daughter had gotten too heavy to hold any longer, but had not wanted to fall asleep herself. Only when she felt something touch her face and woke to find Manuel crouched beside her caressing her face with his rough and raspy hand did she realize that she must have fallen asleep. She sat up abruptly, terrified. Consuelo was still sleeping beside her on the floor, though, safe and sound. Manuel backed away, seeming not to have meant to frighten Maria Soledad, yet leaving her wondering what it was that he had intended.

"Why won't you be my wife?" he asked after a moment, his tone soft and sad.

Maria Soledad was confused by his question. "I am your wife."

Manuel was visibly disheartened by her response, and his reaction made Maria Soledad even more nervous. She did not dare move even one inch, not wanting to be caught off guard by him, but Manuel only continued staring at her in silence for a while longer, then walked off down the hallway and disappeared.

After that night, Maria Soledad became acutely aware of her every move around Manuel. At times, she would be certain that he was staring at her, feeling that she was being watched but not knowing from where. The sense of something unfinished between them kept her on edge.

When she was tucking Consuelo into bed one night a few weeks later, she noticed Manuel step into the doorway of her daughter's room. She looked at him and waited for him to say what he obviously needed to say, wondering if he would finally be able to do so.

"She doesn't look even one bit like me," he said in a calm tone.

Maria Soledad carefully examined his expression, his calmness alleviating nothing for her.

"You have nothing to say to that?" he asked in response to her look, seeming more disappointed than anything else.

Maria Soledad shrugged awkwardly, not knowing how to respond. Manuel had only said what was obvious — Consuelo's skin was a pale creamy colour and her eyes were a clear hazel, and she was far more fair than either of them.

Maria Soledad did not think that actually speaking out the words herself would benefit anybody.

"It's the gossip all over town," he continued after a moment.

Maria Soledad instinctively moved to position herself between Manuel and Consuelo, needing to be sure that there could be no way for him to harm her daughter, but Manuel did not move from where he stood.

"Why did you marry me?" he asked.

"Because you asked me," she replied, wondering if the truth was what he really wanted.

"Have you ever even once tried to love me?"

Maria Soledad did not respond to his question, though she knew that her silence itself spoke loudly of her guilt.

Manuel walked away then, without another word. Maria Soledad could hear his footsteps down the hall, heavy and hollow, until they faded into nothingness.

Maria Soledad saw even less of Manuel after that. He would stay out very late into the night and creep back into the house only after Maria Soledad was certain to have gone to bed. Sometimes in the night, when Manuel likely thought her to be asleep, she could hear him moving about quietly. At times the sounds were accompanied by the faintest of lights, but mostly he remained in the darkness; he seemed to prefer the safety of it, and its calmness, she had come to understand.

Maria Soledad would often wonder what it was that compelled him to movement in the darkness and her curiosity finally got the best of her one night, pushing her to ignore an instinct deep inside her to leave him be. She quietly got out of bed and crept down the hall to his doorway, careful not to step in any of the spots where she knew the floorboards would creak. A small stream of light filtered out of his room and guided her to the tiny crack between the door and the jamb, and when she peeked in through it she was able to see clearly into his room. Manuel stood in front of his open wardrobe door, and hanging inside was her wedding dress. Manuel slowly moved in to the dress and caressed its fabric more tenderly than Maria Soledad would ever have thought he could. He then leaned in and held the dress with immense desire, suddenly starting to cry desperately and uncontrollably. Maria Soledad found it impossible to keep watching him any longer, realizing clearly that neither of them was without guilt — not Manuel, but not she either.

6.

She knew the meaning behind what they were saying was more than the individual words they spoke to each other, but she couldn't figure out what that was. Her parents' loud voices had broken through the quiet of the night and Consuelo had woken with a start. She was still groggy and confused from sleep as she tried to piece together what they were arguing about. After a moment, as she grew more lucid, Consuelo walked out into the hallway where she was able to hear better. She stopped just a short distance from Manuel's partly opened doorway, the light from inside his room seeping out of it and catching her attention.

"One walk after a long hot day is not going to ruin her," Consuelo heard her father tell her mother in an exasperated tone.

"Why are you interfering?"

"She was clearly bored and tired of studying."

"And how would you know that? You've never even spent more than five minutes with her before all this."

"It was clearly written all over her face for anybody with half a mind to see."

Consuelo anticipated the harshness of her mother's response to come, but her mother offered nothing. Instead, silence grew between her parents. Consuelo moved in a bit closer to the doorway to get a better view of the two of them inside the room — she did not want to risk being seen, but felt the need to know why they had suddenly grown so quiet. Her mother was staring at her father, and her father right back; had Consuelo not heard everything that led up to that moment, she might have thought nothing of how they looked at each other, but now it left her with an uneasy sensation.

Consuelo had not expected for her father to take her out earlier that day. She'd always wondered if he even noticed her at all around the house, given how little he ever spoke to her and how little time he spent at home. Consuelo had been sitting at the kitchen table practising her handwriting while her mother prepared supper when Manuel walked in unexpectedly in the middle of the afternoon in his police uniform, asking for some water. His presence made the room suddenly uncomfortable.

"We spent all day outside at the Ross ranch and they sent us home early because of the heat," Manuel told Maria Soledad as he waited for her to pour him his water, noticing the awkward glances between Maria Soledad and her daughter, feeling the need to explain the reason for his intrusion. "The Rosses have been having problems with some of their farmhands."

"Really...?" Maria Soledad said as she handed him the glass.

"I didn't know that one of their sons was a lieutenant in the army," he added.

"That's interesting," Maria Soledad responded, then said nothing more, allowing an awkward silence to fall into the room.

"The *patrón* wasn't sure if his youngest son would amount to anything," Manuel continued. "He said he spent a fortune sending him to the best schools, but he was still having problems with him before they sent him off to the military academy."

"Did you want some more water?" Maria Soledad asked, motioning to his nearly empty glass.

"No, thanks," Manuel responded. "They should have just sent him off to the military academy in the first place," he continued with his original train of thought.

Consuelo found Manuel's lingering presence in the kitchen to have made her mother unusually uneasy. The exchange between the two of them seemed awkward with Manuel insisting on having a conversation when it seemed obvious to Consuelo that her mother wasn't interested in speaking to him. Or, maybe it was the topic that had made her mother uneasy.

"I suppose if you're that rich you can do whatever you want," Maria Soledad said after a while, starting to clean the dishes in the sink.

"You don't have to remind me of that," Manuel replied, his words for some reason stopping the conversation completely.

Consuelo noticed Maria Soledad look up from the sink, though she did not turn to look at Manuel. Maria Soledad stared at the wall in front of her for a few seconds, seeming to need a moment to think. She then put her rag down and walked over to Manuel. "If you're tired, maybe you should have a siesta," she said, taking his empty glass from him. "Supper won't be ready for a while."

It was at that moment that Manuel turned his attention to Consuelo. Consuelo quickly looked back at the exercise book on the table in front of her and started working on her handwriting again, hoping he wouldn't notice that she'd been staring at him.

"Did you want another glass of water?" Consuelo heard her mother ask Manuel.

"No thanks," Manuel replied. From the corner of her eye Consuelo could see that he was still looking at her.

"What are you working on?" he asked.

It was only after a brief moment of silence that Consuelo realized he was talking to her and not her mother. She looked up at him hesitantly, uncertain what to say.

"Is it a secret — ?"

Consuelo hadn't expected the playfulness of his tone.

"She's working on her printing," Maria Soledad answered from behind him.

"What — ?" Manuel turned back to look at Maria Soledad, visibly stunned by her response. "She hasn't even started school yet."

"It's never too early to start."

"She's just a child."

"She's my daughter," Maria Soledad responded. "Of course I know she's a child."

It was only then that Consuelo realized her parents were having an argument; there was nothing unusual in the words they spoke or the tone they used, but the delay between their responses to each other seemed just a bit too long and deliberate.

"Do you want to go for a walk to the plaza before supper?" Manuel asked after a moment, clearly not talking to Maria Soledad, and so Consuelo deduced the offer must have been intended for her.

Consuelo was speechless, not certain how to respond to her father — or even if she should. Regardless, though, he held out his hand for her to take.

"Come on," he said. "Let's get out of your mother's way while she finishes supper."

It was rare for her mother to let her go out of the house in the middle of the day, especially when she hadn't yet finished her lesson. She would normally accompany her mother to the market in the mornings after her father had finished breakfast and left for work and then help her mother get *almuerzo* ready, but after that Consuelo had to work on the reading and writing assignments that Maria Soledad would give her. School was still a year away for her because she hadn't yet turned seven, but her mother had insisted on starting her with some lessons to get her prepared. Maria Soledad had always told her that she hadn't been able to go to school herself and so it was something Consuelo should never take for granted. And for that reason, Consuelo had tried her hardest to focus on her assignments as diligently as she could while her mother did her afternoon chores, but she found that nearly unbearable. She could often hear children from the neighbourhood playing out on the street those afternoons and she wanted so much to be able to join them, but she knew that she would only disappoint her mother if she asked. There was the occasional afternoon when her aunts would come in from the convent in Talca to visit and sometimes Consuelo would accompany them while they did some shopping, but that happened only rarely. Mostly, Consuelo would sit alone at the kitchen table desperately wishing for the time to pass faster.

"All I ever do is cook and clean," her mother had told her just before Manuel had come in that afternoon. "But when you grow up, you can be anything you want."

Her father held her hand as they walked down the street, with a grip firm and secure. For some reason, being in the company of her father alone gave her a greater sense of comfort than she'd ever felt with her mother.

Consuelo could not recall ever having spent time alone with her father before. There were times when they would go out to police family events over the holidays in the summer, but Manuel would mostly spend time with the other officers, away from the women and children. Consuelo didn't have much family on her father's side, either. Her father was from a small town closer to the mountains and his parents had died long ago when an illness had worked its way through the town, leaving many people dead. Manuel had a brother who was also a police officer, but he was stationed in the north and Consuelo had seen him only once briefly, several years ago.

"You must be Consuelo," the police officer said when she opened the door that afternoon. Her mother was ironing some clothes in her bedroom when they'd heard knocking and she'd asked Consuelo to see who it was.

Consuelo wasn't sure how to respond to the man — she wasn't sure if she was supposed to know him, though she didn't recognize him.

"Can you tell Manuel that Ceferino's here to see him," the man said as he stepped into the house, not even waiting to be invited in.

Consuelo nodded and walked down the hallway back to her mother. When she told her mother who it was, Maria Soledad quickly scurried off to Manuel's study to get him. Her father then walked out to the front door and motioned Ceferino into the sitting room, closing the door behind them.

"Who is that?" Consuelo later asked her mother as she watched her prepare tea for them, bringing out the best cups.

"That's your father's brother," Maria Soledad told her. "He's on his way to Antofagasta."

Consuelo caught a glimpse of her father and his brother when Maria Soledad took the tea in. Manuel and Ceferino were both laughing when Maria Soledad opened the door, and that had caught Consuelo's attention. Though she saw very little of her father in general, she couldn't recall ever having seen him seem so light-hearted before. Manuel was always quiet and serious around the house, and his police uniform made him look even more stern. Consuelo could tell that even her mother found her father's demeanour that afternoon unusual, as Maria Soledad smiled at Manuel when he looked up at her laughing, and then continued to watch him, fascinated, while she poured the two men tea.

That afternoon when Manuel took her out for a walk to the plaza, even though her father was still in his police uniform, he carried the same light-hearted air that he'd had when his brother had come to visit.

"Let's get some ice cream cones," Manuel said as they got closer to the plaza. "Just make sure not to mention this to your mother, or we'll both be in trouble," he added, smiling.

Maria Soledad didn't say much to either Consuelo or Manuel when they returned later that afternoon. Normally, Consuelo wouldn't have thought much of silence at the table while they were eating, but that evening even the silence had an edge to it. The silence continued when Consuelo helped her mother clear off the table later and then do the dishes in the kitchen, and she found nothing calm in it at all.

When she finally went to bed that night, Consuelo was certain that whatever had come over her mother would pass by morning. Consuelo had seen Maria Soledad grow upset before, and she would always eventually return to her normal self, if not the next day, then certainly the day after. When she'd woken to find her parents arguing that night, though, Consuelo was left wondering how often they fought when she was asleep, or whether that was the first time it had happened. Consuelo had never seen the two of them arguing that way before, where they challenged each other so directly, and over what seemed to Consuelo to be such a small thing.

"Nobody can say anything against the way I fulfil my duties — I make sure that your clothes are immaculately cleaned and ironed, and that you have three good meals each and every day," Maria Soledad said to Manuel, breaking the silence that had worked its way through them that night. "All I want to do is give my daughter every opportunity in life, so why are you intent on interfering with that?"

"I'm not interfering. A short walk before supper is not interfering."

"She's *my* daughter and I'm the one who decides that."

Suddenly there was silence all over again.

"I have the right to spend time with her," Manuel continued after a moment.

"Fine," Maria Soledad allowed, clearly not pleased at all. "But don't ever get in the way of the opportunities I want her to have. And if you ever even think of laying one finger — "

"Get out!" Manuel yelled out abruptly, cutting off her mother before she had the chance to finish what she was saying.

Maria Soledad didn't move, though. Instead, she just stood there with a self-satisfied smile.

"Get out now!" Manuel said again, this time far colder than before, the harshness of his tone even making Consuelo frightened.

Consuelo didn't have enough time to get back to her room before Maria Soledad stepped out into the hallway. Instead, Consuelo quietly leaned back up against the darkened wall behind her and hoped her mother would not notice her as she passed by. From the shadows, she watched her mother walk towards her bedroom and then abruptly stop. Maria Soledad stood completely still in the hallway for what seemed to Consuelo to be an eternity, staring out the window into the yard and even further into the night beyond. Finally, as suddenly as she had stopped, her mother continued on her way down the hall, not having noticed Consuelo at all.

After Maria Soledad had closed her bedroom door, Consuelo waited for a bit before moving, needing to be sure that her mother would not suddenly reappear. Only when she was convinced that there was absolute stillness in the house did Consuelo move again. She quietly walked over to the window where her mother had stopped, curious to see what it was that had caught her attention. Consuelo scanned the darkness outside, but all she could see were the tops of houses and trees, which suddenly ended off in the distance with the deep dark air that sat above the ocean. Beyond the ocean, she could see nothing at all. Consuelo couldn't decide what it was that her mother had been staring it. Perhaps it was that emptiness above the ocean that had caught her attention, but she couldn't be certain — there was so little about her mother that she ever understood.

7.

"What are we waiting for?" he asked, breaking the silence that had come to surround them.

"Shhh — !" Consuelo hushed him quickly. "Watch this," she whispered after a moment, abruptly running out into the field.

As she ran through the grass, dozens of butterflies suddenly flew up out of it, swarming around Consuelo before fluttering off in different directions.

"See," she said, running back to Angel after the last butterfly had flown off. "What did I tell you?"

Angel had smiled at her the first day of school. He was the first one who had, and with it had offered her a deep sense of relief. Consuelo had developed a growing sense of uneasiness that morning on her way to school. The whole summer before, she couldn't wait for that day to come. Even though she would still have to study like she did at home, at least in school she would be able to meet friends without worrying that it would upset her mother. But on the morning that school finally did start, a sense of dread worked its way into her as she began to worry about the day that lay ahead of her — what if nobody wanted to be friends with her? Consuelo's sense of anxiety grew when she stepped into the classroom that morning to find herself surrounded by so many new and unfamiliar faces. It was then that Angel had smiled.

Angel was a scrawny little boy, the twists and kinks of his thick dark hair neatly combed back but revealing hints of themselves regardless. He sat a bit behind all the other children who were already in the classroom, and when Consuelo noticed the empty desk beside him, she quickly made her way to it.

"You live just around the corner from me," he said in a matter-of-fact tone as she sat down. "Why don't you ever come out and play?"

"My mother won't let me," she told him.

"That's what my mother said," he said, nodding his head, Consuelo's answer having confirmed to him what he seemed to already know. "My mother says your mother thinks she's better than everybody else."

"How would your mother know that?" she asked, slightly offended but more curious than anything else.

"My mother's your aunt."

Consuelo looked at Angel, confused. "But neither of my aunts have any children. They're both nuns."

"My father is one of your mother's brothers," he clarified.

"Oh," Consuelo said after a moment, it not having occurred to her before that she had more aunts than just her mother's twin sisters. She stared at Angel curiously then. "You're my cousin?"

Angel nodded in response.

"I didn't realize I had any," Consuelo continued.

"You have lots," he told her. Almost as an afterthought, he told her his name: "I'm Angel."

"Why does Dad get to go to church and we have to stay at home?" Consuelo asked her mother the following Sunday, after she'd heard the familiar echoing sound of the door closing shut behind her father on his way out alone.

She'd found her mother in the kitchen, where she always was. Maria Soledad was washing the dishes from the morning's breakfast when Consuelo asked her the question. "Your father *chooses* to go to church," she replied, as if that should have clarified the issue.

From the hallway, Consuelo watched her mother continue with her chores. After Maria Soledad finished washing the dishes, she dried each one of them by hand and tucked it into its proper storage place. She did not seem to give her daughter a second thought even though Consuelo still stood there looking at her.

"Angel said I have a lot of cousins," Consuelo blurted out after a moment.

"And how would this Angel know that?" her mother asked, only half paying attention to her.

"Because he said he's one himself."

Maria Soledad stopped to think for a moment, then continued with her work again. "That's right, he is one of your cousins," she confirmed.

"Why haven't I ever met any of them?" Consuelo asked.

"Why haven't you met any of your cousins — ?" her mother asked. "This whole town is full of our relatives. Everybody you bump into on the street is related to us one way or another."

"Angel's mother says you think you're better than everybody else," Consuelo pushed, wanting for her mother to react, wanting some emotion from her.

"Well, maybe this Angel should mind his own business," her mother replied coolly, but still calmly, and not at all in the way Consuelo had thought she would.

"Angel said they all go to church on Sundays, and we're the only ones who don't," Consuelo continued.

Maria Soledad finally stopped her work and looked directly at her daughter. "So that's what this is all about?"

"Why can't I go with them?" she finally blurted out. "Why do I always have to stay here with you?"

"If that's what you want — fine," her mother responded. "Believe me though, you're only going to be bored by the whole thing."

The following Sunday, Consuelo carefully put on her new dress, the one her grandmother had made for her seventh birthday but which Maria Soledad had not allowed her to wear before that day. "You can't just wear such a nice dress without a good reason," she had told Consuelo before taking the dress away almost in the very moment it had been given to her, putting in a trunk packed with mothballs.

"Look at you!" her father said when Consuelo walked out into the hallway that morning with the dress on. "Don't you look pretty."

Consuelo noticed her mother give Manuel a quick scolding look in response, perhaps thinking that Consuelo wasn't watching, but her father clearly disregarded it. Instead, he turned all his attention back to his daughter.

"Come on, Consuelo," he said, holding out his hand for her to take. "Let's get out of your mother's way."

When they arrived at the church, Manuel led Consuelo to where Angel was already sitting. He was surrounded by other family members, she assumed, though she only recognized her grandmother and grandfather.

"Well, will you look at this," her grandmother said, stunned by Consuelo's presence. "How did you manage to convince Maria Soledad to let her come?" she asked Manuel.

"Consuelo asked to come," Manuel responded.

Then, just as her father was speaking, a sudden hush came over the church and everybody turned to look off to the front corner. Consuelo followed in the direction of the looks and saw a priest, dressed in a flowing white robe, come in from the side door. He was followed by four altar boys who rang bells as they walked along behind him to the altar.

At first, every part of the mass captivated Consuelo and she absorbed every detail of it, but when the priest started talking, he continued with his sermon for far longer than she was capable of paying attention and the novelty of the experience was soon replaced by boredom. She would glance at Angel every now and then, but his gaze was fixed off to nowhere she could discern. Consuelo wondered if he might have been purposely ignoring her, but then she realized that he was just as bored as she was.

When the people in the church suddenly all stood up, Consuelo was relieved that the mass was finally over. She started to follow her father up off the pew, but Angel motioned for her to stay put.

"It's not over yet," Angel quietly said to her when she looked at him. "They're just going for communion now," he explained.

Consuelo noticed that it was only the adults and older children who got up, and they all followed in a line to the front. The priest put a wafer in each of their mouths and held up a goblet for them to drink from. The people in line then looped back along the side aisles to return to their seats.

"Will it be over soon?" Consuelo asked Angel, careful to keep her voice to a whisper.

"No, not really," he replied. "I told you that you weren't missing anything," he added, seeming to sense her frustration.

"But you said everybody came."

"No. I said everybody *had* to come," he clarified.

"So, how was it?" Maria Soledad asked Consuelo the minute she returned home with her.

Consuelo thought that if she didn't make eye contact with her mother, she could pretend not to have heard her and not have to respond, but she had no such luck.

"Aren't you going to answer your mother?" Manuel asked after a moment had passed.

Consuelo looked up at her father in disbelief, surprised that he would be siding with her mother and not her, when it was quite apparent that Maria Soledad never sided with him.

"Consuelo — !" he said in a reprimanding tone after another moment of silence had passed.

She glared at her father bitterly, then turned to her mother. "It was nice," Consuelo told her, not wanting to allow her mother the satisfaction of being right, yet knowing that her mother knew the truth regardless.

Consuelo had come across the field filled with butterflies later that Sunday afternoon. She'd been so disappointed by that day and longed to be alone, away from everybody and everything. Most especially, she'd wanted to be away from her mother.

Her father had let her go out and play before *almuerzo* on the condition that she not go farther than the plaza, but Consuelo hadn't been in the mood for obeying him and instead continued down one of the dusty roads until she found herself just outside of town, beside that field. It was peaceful and remote there, with tall grasses she could hide herself in, and so she'd walked into it. It was then that the butterflies had first fluttered up around her and instantly delighted her. She'd wanted to show Angel that place right away, but it was not until the following Sunday when they'd managed to head out there together, after Manuel had given them permission to go to the plaza for an ice cream cone.

"I didn't know there were so many butterflies here," Angel said.

"You could catch some of them, couldn't you?" Consuelo asked.

"I don't know. Maybe if I had a net," Angel replied hesitantly, seeming uncomfortable with the idea. "Why would you want to do that?"

"Don't you think they're beautiful?"

"But why would you want to catch one?" he asked again.

"Maybe I can have my own butterfly case," she said. "Like the one in the science room at school."

"The glass case with the butterflies pinned down?" Angel asked, seeming not to have expected that. "We'd better head back before your parents start to worry," he continued after a moment before walking off, neither giving Consuelo the opportunity to respond nor waiting for her.

"Maybe I can get one of the other boys in the class to help me," Consuelo said as she rushed up after him.

Angel stopped and looked back at her. "No, I can do it," he said.

Angel seemed disappointed with himself in the moment he spoke those words, but that was not Consuelo's concern.

From inside the house, Consuelo watched Angel and her father out in the yard the following weekend, cutting and nailing the wood together for the case to hold her butterflies. As she watched the two of them, she felt unusually lonely. After she'd woken that morning, she'd found Manuel eating breakfast alone in the darkened kitchen — something her mother would never have allowed.

"You can fix yourself whatever you want for breakfast," he told her. "Your mother went to Talca to visit her sisters at the convent."

She hadn't thought much about it then, so early in the morning, but as she sat alone inside the house watching her father and Angel, it soon occurred to her that she couldn't think of any other time when Maria Soledad had gone to visit any of her family members — not even once. When her aunts were in town, they would come by first to see Maria Soledad and then leave for their parents' house, but Maria Soledad would never accompany them there. And, Consuelo couldn't remember any other time when her mother had, in turn, gone to visit her sisters.

When Consuelo had asked Manuel a few days earlier to help her and Angel make the case for her butterflies, Maria Soledad became so deeply upset that even Consuelo, with all her experience with her mother's moods, was caught off-guard.

"How could it ever have occurred to you to keep dead butterflies in a case?"

The way her mother described it made Consuelo feel as though she were doing something perverse.

"They have one in school and it *does* look beautiful," she explained herself.

"Nothing that's locked up is beautiful, let alone something that's dead."

Consuelo stared at her mother, stunned by her words.

"You're the one who always harps on her to take more of an interest in her school work — and now that she does, you get upset with her?" Manuel cut in, to Consuelo's relief. "That's just so typical of you, woman."

Maria Soledad very slowly turned toward Manuel and gave him an incredibly fierce and cold look. Consuelo found it eerie, especially because of how controlled it was. But if Manuel had found it as disturbing, he did not let on. Instead, he met her mother's stare directly, without backing down. After the longest of moments, Maria Soledad finally looked down to the ground and closed her eyes. Consuelo thought at first that her mother was going to blink, given the lightness and speed with which she'd closed her eyes, but she did not open them again for several seconds. Consuelo wondered what her mother could have been thinking in that moment, what could have been passing through her mind to give her the sense of absolute steadiness that Consuelo felt from her when she finally did open her eyes. Maria Soledad pushed back her chair then and walked away without another word.

"Here it is," her father announced as he walked into the house after having spent several hours out in the work shed with Angel, who followed in right after him, holding the finished butterfly case.

Consuelo rushed over to have a look. The three butterflies that Angel had caught her were all neatly lined up with their wings open, each of them catching the light with their coats and reflecting it out magically.

"Consuelo — aren't you forgetting something?" her father asked.

Consuelo looked at Manuel, at first not understanding to what he was referring, but then suddenly remembering what her father had instructed her earlier. "Thank you for all your help, Angel," she said in a well-rehearsed manner, and then gave him a kiss on the cheek.

Angel smiled nervously and his face flushed

Maria Soledad returned home after night had fallen, long after Consuelo had already gone to bed. Consuelo kept track of her mother's movements in the hallway through the crack of her slightly open bedroom door. Maria Soledad had lit a candle when she'd come in, and she cast a long and dark shadow along the wall as she moved about. After a few minutes had passed, Consuelo's door creaked open and her mother emerged from that shadow to give her daughter a good-night kiss. Consuelo quickly closed her eyes in the instant she heard her door open, and then opened them again only after she heard her mother head back out again.

Consuelo watched Maria Soledad carefully and quietly close the bedroom door behind her as she walked out, shutting out along with it the light from the hallway that had come in with her. Consuelo looked at the door for another moment before turning back to look at the butterfly case on the night table beside her. She reached out to touch the glass cover of it and then traced her finger along its wooden edges; the cold feeling of it did not satisfy her.

8.

As Consuelo brushed her hair, she could hear her parents arguing farther off down the hall. Though she wasn't able to make out their exact words, she knew they were fighting about the date Manuel had planned for her for that evening. The last date Manuel had arranged for her had been dreadfully boring. Her date spent the whole time talking about things that were happening halfway around the world, about men walking on the moon and about how there was so much tension in the world that it seemed on the verge of exploding — it had been just like spending an afternoon with Angel, only she'd gotten dressed up for the occasion. This time, Manuel had set her up with the son of another police officer recently stationed in town.

When Consuelo and her father arrived at Juan's house later that Saturday afternoon, they were greeted by loud music coming from farther inside the house. Juan met them at the door and Consuelo was a bit surprised to see that he was a small, skinny man, not at all like her father.

"Why don't you sit here?" Juan suggested, opening the sitting room door for them and motioning them in. "It'll be a lot quieter."

Consuelo followed her father in and took the seat right beside him.

"Felix was rather upset when he found out I'd accepted a commission here and that we were moving just before his last year of high school," Juan told Manuel. "He'd been asking for a radio for such a long time so I thought I would get him one to smooth things over, but who knew the thing would be so loud?"

Juan smiled at Consuelo. "I was hoping to find him a reason to stop spending so much time in his room and get him out of the house every now and then."

When Juan stopped speaking all that could be heard in the room was the blaring music, even with the door closed. Juan got up and opened the door.

"Son, will you turn that thing down," he yelled as he poked his head out the door, but to no avail. "I'll be back in a moment," he said, glancing back at the two of them before heading out the door and disappearing down the hall.

Consuelo and her father waited in the room for some time before the music finally stopped.

"Maybe his son doesn't want to go out," Consuelo whispered to her father, scared to speak any louder in case somebody else in the house could hear.

"Nonsense," Manuel said, taking her hand. "Who wouldn't want to spend an afternoon with a girl as pretty as you?"

Consuelo managed a nervous smile back to her father; that wasn't what she'd meant, but she didn't want to bother to explain herself either.

Just then, Juan returned to the room with his son following right behind him. In that moment when Consuelo first saw Felix, she was completely mesmerized, never having seen anybody as beautiful as him before.

"Felix — Sergeant Manuel Hernandez works with me," Juan said.

As Felix shook her father's hand, Consuelo could not help but stare at his sharp, cold blue eyes. They were like no colour she'd ever seen before. Juan's eyes were also blue, but they were darker, and not nearly as forceful.

"Consuelo — ?"

She suddenly noticed that her father had been talking to her and she turned to look at him.

"Felix will walk you back home before supper," he told her before heading out.

After Manuel had left, Consuelo wasn't certain what to do next.

"Felix," Juan said, still holding the door open from when her father had left. "Why don't you take Consuelo out to the plaza for a walk like we talked about?"

"I still can't believe how small this place is!" Felix told Consuelo after they sat down on a bench in the plaza. "I always thought that Chillán was about as small as a place could get."

"I know what you mean," Consuelo responded after a moment, feeling that she should say something, but not certain what.

"You've been to Chillán?"

"No, but I've heard people talk about it," she explained, hoping she didn't sound foolish.

"I can't wait until school's finished," Felix continued. "I'll be out of here in no time then."

"Your father's commission is for just one year?" Consuelo asked, finding that unusual.

"Who cares about that? As soon as I'm done school, I'm heading out to Santiago."

"That's where I'm thinking about going, too."

Felix turned and looked at her. "Really?" he asked in disbelief.

"Really," Consuelo said, mustering up a confident tone. "I'm planning on going to university there," she added as an afterthought, hoping it would make her sound more convincing.

The truth was that Angel was the one who was planning to go to university in Santiago, not her. Just the thought of continuing with years of classes after high school made Consuelo cringe. As it was, it was only with Angel's help that she was able to get grades good enough to satisfy her mother, and she longed for the day when that would finally come to an end. That whole afternoon, though, Consuelo was left with the feeling that Felix considered her inconsequential and she would have said just about anything to try to convince him that she was anything but that.

"Pepe saw you with some guy in the plaza the other day," Angel said as he lay on the sand, his tone seeming to Consuelo to be purposefully casual, as though he wanted not to appear overly curious.

Consuelo had found Angel on the beach that afternoon, where he would normally go to read the newspaper. He had so many brothers and sisters and his family lived in such a small house that he wasn't able to get any reading done there, so he'd go down to the beach when the weather was nice. Consuelo knew her father had to work late that day and she wasn't especially eager to be with her mother at home alone, so she'd decided to spend the afternoon with Angel instead.

"Felix's father was just commissioned in town and my dad wanted me to spend some time with him to make him feel more at home here," Consuelo told him as she sat down beside him.

"Another one of your father's set-up dates," Angel commented.

"I guess," Consuelo replied. "But Felix is very interesting."

"Interesting — ?" Angel repeated, but then left it at that, leaving Consuelo uncertain as to what he'd meant.

"He's from Chillán and he has his own radio," Consuelo explained, feeling the need to justify herself. "He's also very good-looking," she added after a moment, for some reason not being able to stop herself from telling Angel that.

"I see," Angel said, then continued reading his newspaper.

Consuelo stared at Angel for a moment as silence grew between them — she was disappointed that he'd left it at that and hadn't asked her another question.

"I've been thinking I should probably try to get into a university in Santiago," she said after a while.

"Really?" Angel asked, looking up at her again. "Since when have you been interested in going to university?"

"You're the one who keeps telling me I should keep my options open."

"It's going to take more than a wish for you to get into a university there," he responded. "But at least if you try to get good grades, you can probably get into a university in Concepción."

"But Santiago's the place to be, isn't it?"

Angel examined Consuelo's expression then, visibly suspicious. "Where did you hear that?"

"I don't know," Consuelo replied, shrugging. "Maybe from Felix," she finally allowed after Angel continued looking at her waiting for a response.

"Oh, well, then it must be," Angel replied.

Consuelo wondered if he'd meant to berate her with his words, but then decided that couldn't be the case because Angel was simply not capable of that.

Consuelo had to rush to catch up to Felix after classes ended that first day of school. When she'd bumped into him earlier in the day, he seemed not to have remembered her. Consuelo had always stood out with her light features and her clear hazel eyes and, even though she hadn't thought much about the way she looked when she was younger, it had become evident to her when she started high school that the boys paid far more attention to her than they did the other girls. When she saw Felix in the hallway earlier, though, he walked right by her without even so much as a smile of recognition. Consuelo had turned to say hello, but even then he only acknowledged her with a quick glance back and nothing more. The way he'd reacted made Consuelo feel embarrassed, but at least nobody else around them seemed to have noticed his slight.

For the rest of the day, Consuelo had tried to convince herself that he was not worth her concern, but then would find herself wondering where he was and hoping that she might bump into him again. She even began to think that he was certain to have an explanation for his earlier behaviour — perhaps the newness of the school had distracted him. She'd kept an eye out for Felix between her classes, but she hadn't caught another glimpse of him until the end of the day, just as she started walking back home.

"Felix — !" she called out as she rushed to catch up to him.

"Oh, hi — " he said, turning around curiously but visibly losing interest when he noticed it was her.

There was an awkward moment of silence as Felix looked at Consuelo waiting for her to say something more. Consuelo, though, was completely unprepared for that moment, not having planned anything beyond catching up to him and getting his attention.

"Did you need something?" he finally asked after a while.

"I was wondering if maybe I could go listen to your radio this afternoon," Consuelo managed to piece together.

"I don't think my mother would like it if I brought somebody over unannounced."

"No, of course not," Consuelo said, trying to hide as much of her disappointment as possible, not wanting him to see that.

"I'll see you around then," Felix said before continuing off again, leaving Consuelo standing on the street alone.

"Did you want to go out for an ice cream?" her father asked her after they finished supper that evening.

"No," Consuelo replied. "I have a lot of school work to do."

"They gave you homework already on your first day?"

"No," Consuelo answered. "I just thought I should try to get ahead in my studies so that I have a chance of getting into university in Santiago."

"Santiago — ?" Manuel asked, visibly surprised. "Why would you want to go there?

"Isn't that where all the good universities are?"

"Concepción has a very good university," he told her.

"Consuelo's right," Maria Soledad interrupted, stepping into the room in that moment, having been listening from the kitchen. "The university in Concepción isn't as good as the ones in Santiago."

"But she'll be able to pick anything she wants to study there, and that's unlikely in Santiago," Manuel responded to her mother.

"It certainly wouldn't hurt Consuelo to try her best and see where it gets her, though. Don't you agree, Manuel?"

"There's nothing at all wrong with the university in Concepción," her father insisted again. "And Concepción's a lot safer than Santiago, not to mention a lot closer to here. I don't know why you would want to send your daughter so far away."

"You're the one who always lets her do whatever she wants," Maria Soledad replied. "So why is it a problem now when what she wants is to study harder?"

"That has nothing to do with it, and you know it. Santiago's a mess."

"If it were up to you, you'd have her stay a little girl forever, wouldn't you?"

Manuel got up abruptly from the table, clearly flustered by Maria Soledad. "Why do you always have to contradict me?" he asked and then left.

"Your father's right," Angel told Consuelo a few days later when they were sitting in the plaza. "Santiago is a mess right now, and it's going to spill over to the rest of the country for sure."

"How is it a mess?"

"You really don't know?" Angel asked, visibly surprised.

Consuelo just shrugged her shoulders, not certain what it was that he thought she should know.

"There's a grass-roots movement going on right now. People are finally standing up to make Chile a true democracy," Angel told her.

"But Chile's already a democracy," Consuelo said, certain that Angel would have already known that.

"On the books it is, but the rich still run everything. Everybody should be able to have a voice in the country — not just the wealthy."

"Oh," Consuelo said, still not really understanding, but not caring to understand either. "Does that mean you don't want to go to Santiago now?"

"Are you kidding? There's no way I'm going to miss being a part of the history that's being made."

Just then, Consuelo noticed Felix pass by with some boys from school, the ones who had bad reputations.

"Isn't that the guy you were talking about — your new friend, the 'interesting' one?" Angel asked, having noticed Felix as well.

"Felix — ? He's nothing special," she replied, trying hard to make it look as though that were actually the case.

"I'll say he's nothing special — it looks like the only thing he's interested in is finding a dark, quiet space to get high."

"You think he does drugs?" Consuelo asked.

"Why else would he be hanging around those guys?"

"But his father's a police officer," she said.

Angel looked at Consuelo curiously. "Maybe your father's right after all, maybe Santiago isn't really a good place for you to be."

Consuelo continued to watch Felix as he walked farther off down the street with his friends and finally disappeared around a corner. Even after he'd so obviously ignored her, there was something about him she found so absolutely spellbinding that she simply could not keep her eyes off him.

9.

"It would appear that some of you have actually discovered the benefits of studying," the math teacher said to the class as he handed back Consuelo her marked test.

Angel had helped Consuelo study almost every single day for close to two weeks before the first exams that fall. She managed to get mainly sixes as scores, though she did get a five and a half in history because there were too many names and dates to have to remember. Her grades weren't nearly as good as Angel's, who managed to get even a few perfect sevens, but they were high enough to put her among the top of the class and would also be good enough to get her into university in Santiago if she managed to keep them up for the rest of the year.

Consuelo hadn't expected the teacher's comment that afternoon, though, as he handed out the marked tests to the class, and she instantly flushed with embarrassment as all the other students turned to look at her. She was concerned what Felix would think, but he sat a few rows behind her and she was unable to see him. After a moment, after everybody had finally stopped looking at her, Consuelo stole a quick glance back at Felix, unable to resist her curiosity any longer. All he was doing, though, was writing on the piece of paper in front of him; if he had noticed anything of what had just happened, he didn't let on.

When Consuelo turned back, she noticed Angel looking at her. He quickly turned away when he saw that she'd noticed him. She glanced over at him a while later, but he was staring ahead to the front of the class. Consuelo didn't notice him look at her again, and when the class was over he quickly left without saying a word to her.

"Consuelo," she heard somebody call out behind her.

She turned around to find Felix walking towards her.

"I didn't know you were such a good student," he said.

"I have to be, to get into university in Santiago," she replied, trying to keep a confident tone that would not betray how nervous she was around him.

"Maybe you want to come over some time and help me study."

Consuelo tried to gauge if she'd understood his tone correctly. She glanced over to the door where Angel had just left — there was no sign of him. For some reason, she needed to be sure that he was not watching before responding.

"Sure," she said looking back at Felix. "I'd like that."

Felix turned on the radio as soon as they walked in. Everything was strewn around in his room — clothes and magazines scattered all over the floor and even some dirty dishes in the corner. Felix closed the door behind her, then stretched out on his bed and lit up a cigarette.

"Did you want one?" he asked, holding out the pack for her.

Consuelo just looked at the cigarettes, uncertain how to respond; she had never smoked before, but did not want Felix to know that.

"Why don't you sit down?" he said after a moment.

Consuelo looked around trying to figure out where exactly she could sit or put her books down, but could not find one open spot.

"There really isn't much room here to study," she said.

"Right here," Felix replied, motioning to the spot beside him on his bed.

Consuelo looked to where Felix was pointing — she desperately wanted to sit beside him but was so nervous that she found herself unable to move. Felix suddenly took her hand, though, and pulled her back to take a seat. He took the books from her hands and set them down on the floor, then started to run his fingers through her hair.

"Relax," he whispered in her ear as he moved in closer to her.

When Felix started kissing her, Consuelo had not anticipated how it would feel — all she felt was the sensation of being smothered by him. Felix held her tightly without giving her the chance to stay there willingly, but she fought her own instinct to try to push away from him. She made herself bear the roughness of his touch and the force he used to lead her through every motion, reminding herself just how much she had wanted for that to happen.

Later, Consuelo picked up her things from the floor as Felix sat smoking a cigarette. He did not say even one word to her as she finished dressing and headed for the door. Even when she looked back at him just before leaving, Felix still didn't even glance at her. An immense sensation of nausea washed over Consuelo as she walked home alone and she was unable to shake the feeling of being smothered still by the smell of Felix left on her body. She wanted nothing more in that moment than to rid herself of that feeling as it clung to her, but was unable, no matter what she thought of or how fast she walked.

"Consuelo, is that you?" Maria Soledad called out from down the hall as she stepped into the house, the loud creak of the front door opening having given her away.

"Yes," she responded quickly to her mother, hoping that would be sufficient for her and that there would be nothing more — but then she saw Maria Soledad walking down the hallway towards her.

"You're home late," her mother commented. "Were you off studying with Angel again?"

Consuelo wasn't prepared for her mother's question and wasn't sure how she should answer, worried that Maria Soledad would see through her lie if she made something up in that moment.

"Well, you'd better hurry up and get yourself cleaned up for supper before your father gets here," Maria Soledad continued after having studied her daughter's expression for a moment.

Consuelo took the opportunity and rushed off to her bedroom, where she quickly took off all her clothes, letting them pile up on the floor beneath her. She grabbed some clean clothes from her dresser and put them on, but they didn't feel comfortable either, no matter how much she adjusted them, and so she pulled them off, too. Consuelo finally put on her nightgown and climbed into bed. She curled herself up into a tiny little ball underneath the covers and was able to find at least a small bit of relief that way.

"Supper's ready," her mother said, popping her head into Consuelo's bedroom a little while later.

"I'm not hungry," Consuelo told her.

"What's wrong?" Maria Soledad asked, stepping into the room. "Aren't you feeling well?"

"I'm just tired."

Maria Soledad reached over to touch her daughter's forehead, measuring for a fever. Consuelo had not expected her to do that, but the coolness of her mother's hand against her skin gave her a deep sense of comfort — the very thing she'd been unable to find for herself. Maria Soledad moved her hand away as quickly as she'd placed it on her, and with it took that comfort away.

Consuelo looked up at her mother, wanting to be able to ask her to touch her again, to comfort and caress her the way she used to when she was a little girl, whenever she'd hurt or nick herself. Consuelo wished desperately for her mother to make everything around them in the world vanish, but she was unable to put her thoughts into words, unable to find words sufficient to erase all that had come between them.

"I just need some rest," Consuelo finally said, turning around in her bed, turning her back to her mother.

After a while, Consuelo heard her door squeak shut and she knew that her mother was gone.

Consuelo stayed home from school for the rest of the week, ill. That night before she finally returned to school, she carefully studied the image of herself in the bathroom mirror, needing to be certain that there was nothing visibly different about her. Her parents hadn't seemed to notice anything, at least nothing that they'd mentioned, but Consuelo still worried that something in the way she looked or the way she held herself would give her away. In the bathroom mirror, though, her face was exactly as she'd remembered — a greyness had not grown over it, nor was there even the smallest change. As she looked at her reflection, Consuelo found it curious that even though she felt herself to have changed in such a profound way, not even the tiniest hint of that was visible from the outside.

"Are you feeling better?" Maria Soledad asked Consuelo as she passed by the kitchen on the way back to her room.

"A bit," she replied.

Her mother smiled at her before returning to her work in the kitchen.

Consuelo watched her mother as she continued with her work, at her face and the expression she carried on it. It occurred to Consuelo only in that moment that perhaps her mother's expression, too, gave away very little about herself. Consuelo thought of the small locked chest her mother kept in the storage room off the side of the house — the contents of it were a mystery to Consuelo, but she knew that it must have been something incredibly precious to her mother because not even her father would touch it.

Consuelo had first discovered the trunk when she was a little girl — it was in a far corner of the storage room, neatly covered in a white sheet that was completely free of dirt and dust, and for that reason stood out from everything else around it. When her father found her starting to uncover it, he quickly stopped her.

"Leave that alone, Consuelo!" he said curtly, leaving her no room to question him, and so she'd returned the sheet back to its place, her curiosity unsated.

It was only years later that she realized the trunk belonged to her mother. Consuelo had woken up parched one night and started to head to the kitchen for a glass of water. When she stepped out of her bedroom, she noticed her mother walking farther off down the hallway, towards the back door. Consuelo instinctively stopped in that moment, careful not to make any noise or move in any way that would draw attention to herself in the darkened hallway; she was not certain why, but she felt that was what she should do. Through the window, Consuelo could see Maria Soledad walk out the back door and head into the storage room. After her mother closed the door behind her, it was only the light that streamed out from the small crack under the door that gave away that she was in there.

As she looked out the window, Consuelo wondered what it was that her mother had needed to get in the middle of the night and was curious to see what she would return with. After some time had passed without her mother having come back out, though, Consuelo realized that Maria Soledad hadn't gone to get something, but rather to see something; it was then that it occurred to her that the trunk and whatever was inside of it must have been her mother's. There were times later throughout the years when Consuelo had found herself alone in the house and with the opportunity to study the trunk further, but she sensed deeply that she was better off not knowing what it contained.

"Did you want something to eat?" her mother asked Consuelo now, as she still stood in the kitchen doorway.

"No, I'm not hungry," Consuelo replied before continuing on her way, pushing back the curiosity that had come over her and offering to her mother the same thing that she herself wanted — her privacy intact.

When Consuelo walked through the school corridor the next morning on her way to her first class, some of the other students turned to look at her as she walked by. She tried to reassure herself that their glances were nothing out of the ordinary, but then she came up to the leering stares and snickers of Felix's friends. Felix's back was turned to her, but he glanced over following his friends' looks and nudges. He looked at Consuelo only briefly, though, offering her not even a smile or look of recognition before turning back to his friends. Consuelo was left paralyzed with embarrassment and did not know what to do next.

"I was beginning to think you were on your deathbed," she heard Angel say from behind her, and Consuelo quickly turned back to look at him, anxious to move away from Felix and his friends with some sense of dignity.

"I stopped by your house the other day, but your mother said you weren't up to seeing anybody," Angel continued.

"I wasn't feeling very well," she said. "But I've gotten over that."

Consuelo stole a quick look back at Felix from the corner of her eye when she was certain that Angel wouldn't notice — Felix was still talking with his friends and didn't seem to have caught any of her and Angel's conversation. For that reason, Felix caught her unprepared when he ran up to her as she was walking home from school. She turned curiously when she heard somebody rushing up behind her, but quickly turned forward again when she noticed it was Felix, certain she wasn't the reason he was in a hurry.

"Aren't you going to wait for me?" she heard him say, and her heart sank. "I missed you all last week," he said when he finally reached her.

"What — ?" Consuelo simply could not understand Felix, the inconsistencies of his behaviour leaving her profoundly confused.

"What happened to you?" he asked, moving her hair away from her face and mesmerizing her all over again.

Consuelo did not understand how Felix was able to control so much of how she felt with just one look. She wanted to be able to move away from him and break his control, but something deep within her needed to enjoy the closeness of him.

"What about this morning?" Consuelo dared ask.

"With my friends — ?"

"You didn't even say one word to me," she said.

"You don't expect me to spend every moment of the day with you, do you?" he asked, suddenly making her feel silly. "You're a very beautiful woman, Consuelo — how could you feel so insecure about yourself?"

After softly kissing her, Felix finally walked off, leaving Consuelo to sort through all the contradictory feelings that welled up in her. As she watched Felix walk down the street and disappear around the corner, she realized that he had not offered to walk her home, nor had he even glanced back at her once after leaving her there alone. Consuelo wondered if she really had misinterpreted his behaviour earlier that morning, but found believing him to be easier. Perhaps he had noticed her walk off to class with Angel and had realized that she was not without boys to pick from — at least, that was what she tried to tell herself.

10.

That evening, her parents were holding a party in her honour — to celebrate both her birthday and her graduation from high school. Her grandmother and twin aunts had arrived shortly after *almuerzo* to help her mother with the final preparations, and just with those three visitors alone the house had become filled with more people than Consuelo could remember ever being there at once before. Hosting in her house seemed to have been reserved for one or two people at a time, and never any more. Consuelo had always thought that her mother just did not like being around other people, but with her twin sisters Consuelo saw a different side of her mother. Around them, Maria Soledad carried an air of lightness that Consuelo had never seen her display with anyone else.

Consuelo watched the women from the parlour where she was seated, while Manuel sat beside her quietly reading the newspaper. After a while, one of her aunts walked over and closed the parlour door; she seemed not to want the commotion from the kitchen to disturb Consuelo or her father, but that was the very thing that had fascinated Consuelo. There was nothing in the silence of the room after the door was closed that remotely interested her, and the occasional sound of the newspaper pages rustling soon came to bore her. She tried to see out the small, draped door window to the hallway and into the kitchen but was only able to catch the briefest fragments of things, with no one image complete enough for her to make sense of or to satisfy her curiosity.

Her twin aunts had followed her mother out of the room shortly after they'd arrived, after Maria Soledad had made up an excuse to explain why she needed to leave so quickly. "I should get back to the kitchen before something burns," she'd said.

In spite of what she'd said, Consuelo knew the real reason why Maria Soledad had rushed out of the room was because Consuelo had upset her and she didn't want to let on about that to her sisters.

When the twins had first arrived that afternoon, Consuelo noticed them quickly hand a package to her mother. She hadn't thought much about that package until Maria Soledad pulled it out later when they were all in the parlour together.

"I got this special order from Chillán just for you," her mother said, holding out the package for Consuelo to take.

Consuelo wasn't surprised to find the package contained a dictionary, even though that was the last thing she wanted. She thanked her mother for it regardless, though, knowing her father would have expected that.

"I have something for you, too," Manuel said then, holding out a small box.

By Maria Soledad's quick glance at the box, it was clear that her mother didn't know anything about it before that moment. Inside, Consuelo found a delicate silver necklace, and she could not contain her delight.

"It's so beautiful!" she said, hugging her father.

Consuelo had never gotten any jewellery before, though some of the girls at school regularly wore earrings and necklaces to class. She'd asked Manuel a few years earlier if she could have a necklace, but he had told her he didn't think it was a good idea. Consuelo had always suspected it was because of Maria Soledad, but her father had never let on.

Consuelo thought nothing more of her reaction to the necklace then, but it was immediately after that when her mother had abruptly left, quickly followed out by the twins. Suddenly, Consuelo had found herself alone in the room with her father.

After finally giving up trying to catch an unobstructed glimpse of the women in the kitchen after the door was closed, Consuelo looked at Manuel for a moment, then picked up the jewellery box and headed back to her room.

"You can wear that necklace tonight if you want," Manuel told her as she stepped out the door. "It's your special night, after all."

Later that evening, Consuelo heard her guests start to arrive as she sat on her bed, but she decided to wait a bit longer before heading out to greet them. She didn't want to be caught in the awkward position of being around a small group of people without having anything to say, and so she waited to be sure that more guests had arrived before joining them.

Consuelo had asked Felix to accompany her that evening. He'd told her he would try to make it, but she was left with the lingering feeling that his words were not an actual indication of intention. She had noticed some of his friends walking down the street towards the plaza when she looked out her window a bit earlier, where she was certain that Felix would be joining them. She had found Felix there a few days earlier, accompanied by some of his friends and some girls.

"I'm heading to Santiago in a few weeks," she told him after he walked over to meet her.

"Yeah, I heard."

"I thought you might want to spend some time together before then," she said.

"Sure, Consuelo, we can do that," Felix replied, smiling and moving his hand in to caress her cheek. "We can spend some time together right now."

He suddenly started kissing Consuelo right there, instantly embarrassing her. She pushed away from him and quickly glanced around to see if anybody else in the plaza other than his friends had seen them — fortunately, it seemed that nobody else had.

"What's the matter?" Felix asked, more as a protest.

"Not here. Not in front of everybody," she replied, not understanding how that couldn't have been obvious to him.

"We can go back to my place," he offered. "My parents are out this evening and won't be back until late."

"Can't we just go for a walk?" Consuelo asked. "Maybe talk a bit."

"Sure, we can do that sometime," Felix answered. "I should get back to my friends," he added after a moment.

Consuelo just nodded then, trying to avoid looking directly at him; she was scared that if she did, she would start to cry, and that was the last thing she wanted him to see.

Still sitting on her bed now, Consuelo heard a soft knocking on her bedroom door and turned to find her grandmother poke her head into the room.

"Consuelo dear," she said. "Your guests are waiting for you."

Consuelo nodded briefly and followed her grandmother out. Just before stepping into the hallway, she caught a glimpse of herself in the mirror — her beautiful dress, her hair done just right and the necklace that glimmered so brilliantly around her neck. But even then, even with everything so perfect, she was still not enough.

"That is a stunning necklace," Felix's mother said as she entered the parlour and greeted Consuelo.

Consuelo noticed Felix's father Juan walk in right after his wife, and for a fraction of a second she let her guard down and let herself hope that Felix had accompanied her parents, but when she looked behind Juan she found nobody.

"So beautiful and so smart, too," Juan said as he walked up to Consuelo. "Felix would have been wise to have followed your example. He's always wanted to go to Santiago, but technical school in Chillán is as far as his grades are going to get him."

Consuelo managed to return a weak smile to Juan before he and his wife stepped further into the room.

"Please don't tell me you're surprised he's not here," Angel said in a condescending tone as he came up to Consuelo, a half-drunk glass of wine in his hand.

Consuelo turned and glared at him, but did not say one word.

"Hey, don't blame me," he said, responding to her look. "It's not like I stopped him from coming."

Consuelo didn't know what came over her in that moment, but she simply didn't care to pretend any more. She walked out of the room then, not at all concerned that she might upset Angel or what her guests would think of her.

Alone in the darkness of her bedroom, Consuelo could hear a variety of things: the floor boards squeaking every now and then from the footsteps of her guests as they moved around; her window shaking slightly as the occasional car drove by the street; and further off, something rhythmic and bassy, so faint that she almost missed it beneath everything else. That sound felt instantly familiar to her, though she could not place it. She closed her eyes and concentrated on the sound until a memory finally revealed itself: a day long ago when her mother had taken her to the beach, when she was just three or four years old. The memory surprised Consuelo because it was something she hadn't ever recalled before, yet in that moment, it became as real to her as if it had just happened. She remembered being overwhelmed by the sudden beating sounds of the waves and turning her head to look as her mother carried her. It was in that moment when she suddenly saw the vastness of the ocean. Consuelo didn't know if that was the first time she had ever seen the ocean, but it was the earliest recollection of it that she had. For some reason, the memory comforted her immensely.

"Consuelo?" her mother called to her from her door in a soft and caring tone.

When Consuelo had first heard the footsteps in the hallway walking closer to her room, she had desperately hoped it was not her father. Consuelo felt a sense of relief when she heard her mother's voice, even though normally she would have found her father to be more comforting.

"What's wrong?" her mother asked as she stepped into the room.

"Nothing," Consuelo replied quietly, still curled up in her bed.

"Your guests are wondering what's happened to you," her mother said. "Your father put a lot of effort into planning this evening."

"I'm tired," Consuelo offered after a brief silence, hoping that would be a sufficient explanation.

Maria Soledad walked farther away into the room after a moment, taking a seat beside Consuelo on her bed. She softly caressed her daughter's face, and Consuelo enjoyed the warmth of her mother's touch.

"If you're tired, then you should rest," her mother said, moving in to kiss Consuelo on the forehead. Consuelo could hear her mother's heart beating as she leaned up against her daughter, and then the sound suddenly stopped as Maria Soledad got up and left the room. Consuelo was then left alone again in the darkness.

Her father held her hand tightly before letting her get onto the train. Angel had already walked up ahead of her to find their seats.

"Let me take them up for you," Manuel offered when Consuelo glanced down at her bags on the platform.

"I'm going to have to carry them by myself the rest of the way," she replied. "I might as well start getting used to that now."

Consuelo gave her father a hug. When she separated from him, he continued holding onto her one hand as if not wanting to let her go.

"Take care of yourself," he said when he finally did let go, after a long moment of silence.

"I will," Consuelo said.

"And study hard so that you'll make your mother proud," he added.

Consuelo smiled at her father before grabbing her bags and stepping up into the train, following in the direction Angel had gone.

That morning, Maria Soledad had accompanied Consuelo and Manuel only as far as the front door, after having woken at the crack of dawn to prepare breakfast for them before their trip to Chillán, where Consuelo and Angel would catch the train to Santiago. The whole week before, Maria Soledad had helped Consuelo prepare for her trip, washing and ironing all her good clothes and helping her pack her bags. There had been little conversation between the two of them, and though there had been nothing unusual in that, for some reason it just was not enough for Consuelo any more — she had wanted her mother to say something to her, anything with meaning beyond the task at hand, but Maria Soledad had offered her nothing at all.

Manuel was loading up the waiting police car with her bags when Consuelo stepped out the front door that morning.

"I've packed food for both you and Angel," her mother told her, handing her a paper-wrapped package. "Your father's going to take you to a restaurant in Chillán for *almuerzo*, so there should be enough food here to last you for the whole trip."

Consuelo nodded her head in acknowledgement, not knowing what to say to her mother.

"Remember to study hard," her mother continued, grabbing hold of Consuelo's hands, but stopping all contact there.

"I will," Consuelo replied.

After a moment of awkwardness, Consuelo turned and got into the car, her father following in right after her. As they drove off, she saw her mother step back into the darkened doorway and become just a shadow. Then, as the car turned the corner, even that shadow disappeared.

Angel and his parents were already waiting at the bus station when Consuelo and her father arrived. After some brief good-byes, the three of them got onto the bus for the first leg of their journey. The bus travelled through the still-darkened streets that morning as it headed out of town, making its way past the school and the plaza before finally heading out onto the highway. She thought it odd, that after all those years and all the memories she'd collected, that leaving would be so simple. Not even the earth shook like it sometimes did early in the morning — that morning everything was quiet and still.

Angel had already found their seats on the train and was storing his bags on the top bin when Consuelo caught up to him. He grabbed her bags without a word when he noticed her and put them up beside his. As the train started to pull out, Consuelo quickly sat down and scanned out the window to the platform below, looking for her father. When she caught sight of him, she slid open the window.

"Dad!" she called out, stretching out her hand towards him.

Manuel stepped forward when he saw her and reached his hand out to touch hers, but Consuelo was only able to feel the briefest touch of his fingers before the moving train separated the two of them. She then waved at him until he was so distant that she could no longer see him — even then she continued waving for a bit longer, waving at the memory of him standing on the platform, watching his daughter leave.

11.

When she first arrived in Santiago, Consuelo was overwhelmed by just how large the city was. It was immense, with buildings larger than she realized even existed, much larger than those even in Chillán, and the streets were filled with commotion at all hours of the day and night. Even the *pensión* where they were staying was much bigger than she had imagined it would be, with a dozen rooms over two floors all opening up into a tiled courtyard in the middle.

"Your rooms are upstairs," *Señora* Carmen said as she led them through the courtyard to the stairs. "The rooms are quieter up there, so you'll have the perfect environment for your studies."

Señora Carmen was an aunt of Angel's mother, but she didn't resemble Angel at all with her straight dark hair and her small frame. It was only because Carmen had agreed to take the two of them in at her *pensión* just a few blocks from the university that Manuel had relented about letting Consuelo go to Santiago.

After Carmen showed Consuelo to her room and left to show Angel his, Consuelo went to the window at the back of the room and opened it to study its view. It was in that moment, with the city spread out before her as far as she could see, that Consuelo started to doubt her decision to move so far away from home, especially when she wasn't sure if she really wanted to continue with her studies. After all the effort to get there, though, she knew going back home now was not really an option.

When Angel walked Consuelo to her classroom the first day of classes, before heading off to his own, she was startled to find a room nearly the size of her high-school gymnasium already half-filled with students.

"Are you sure this is the right place?" she asked Angel. "It seems awfully big to be a classroom."

"It's not so big," Angel said, clearly not having noticed how intimidated Consuelo felt. "Some of the classrooms are even bigger than this one."

"Oh," Consuelo said, and left it at that.

Consuelo had wanted to ask him to stay with her and accompany her during her class like he had throughout high school, but she knew enough not to. Angel had talked for days about nothing more than how much he was looking forward to his classes, and she was sure that asking him to stay with her would have only upset him.

"I'll meet you at the benches out front after classes are finished," Angel told her. "But, remember that my last class finishes a half hour after yours, so you're going to have to wait for a bit."

After Angel left, the classroom around Consuelo filled up quickly, growing with much movement and chatter, but then suddenly quiet moved in as the professor arrived and set himself up at the front. The professor immediately launched into his lecture, catching Consuelo unprepared, not sure what she should be doing. She noticed the other students around her open up their notebooks and start to take notes, and so she decided to follow their lead, though she wasn't really sure if she was writing down the right things or if she even really understood what the professor was saying.

The rest of the classes that day were just as confusing to Consuelo as the first one, and being surrounded by so many students but yet having no one to talk to left her feeling more and more alone. When the end of the day finally came she could barely wait to see Angel again, but her excitement quickly started to wane after the half hour he'd told her to wait had come and gone without him arriving. Consuelo started to wonder if she was waiting in the right place, but when she glanced around her, the only benches she could see in the front of the building were where she was seated. With every minute that passed, Consuelo grew more and more uneasy because she did not know what could have happened to Angel or what she should do — but finally, almost a half hour after he said he would meet her, she noticed him rush out the front door towards her. Consuelo quickly turned back to face the other way, not wanting Angel to see that she'd been looking for him.

"I'm sorry I'm so late," Angel said as he rushed up to her. "I started talking with some of the other students after class and I completely lost track of the time."

"That's all right," Consuelo responded curtly, even though the truth was that his explanation had only served to make her more upset. "I was just reviewing my class notes anyway — it's never too early to get a head start, is it?"

Angel studied her expression for a moment. "I really am sorry," he said, having correctly sensed the falseness of her words.

"I said it's all right," Consuelo replied, aware that her tone was just as curt as before.

Before giving Angel a chance to respond, Consuelo quickly gathered up her things and started walking off towards the *pensión*, purposefully making him have to rush to catch up to her. Though she'd been so desperately lonely that whole day without him, letting Angel know that was the last thing her pride would allow her to do, especially when he seemed to have completely forgotten about her.

"There's going to be a get-together Friday night — did you want to go with me?" Angel asked when they finally got back to the *pensión*, just as they reached her bedroom door; the way he'd phrased his words made it perfectly clear to Consuelo that he was going to go, even without her.

"You're going to be talking about politics there, aren't you?" she asked, knowing already that would be the case even as she asked the question, because that was the only thing that ever interested Angel.

"It's not going to be just that," Angel was quick to reply. "There will be a lot of people for us to meet. Maybe you'll even make some new friends."

"I don't know..." Consuelo said, not entirely convinced by his words.

"We can leave the party at any time if you don't feel comfortable."

"Promise?" she asked, still uncertain but not wanting to be left alone in the *pensión* either.

"I promise."

At first, Consuelo was relieved when Mario walked up to her that evening. Angel had wandered off a while earlier after having told her that he was going to the bathroom, but when she looked around a bit later she noticed him talking to a woman off in a corner. It was then that Mario had come up to her.

"What are you studying?" he asked after introducing himself.

"Education."

"Have you been out to the *poblaciones* yet to teach the children there?"

"No, I've only just started my classes," she responded after an awkward moment; Mario had looked at her waiting for her response after he'd asked his question, but she wasn't entirely sure that she'd understood it.

"Everybody needs to contribute to the revolution," he said, but his meaning still eluded Consuelo. "It's not enough to just say that we support Allende, we have to show our support by volunteering for the movement."

"I'm really not into politics," Consuelo said, suddenly understanding that was what he was talking about. "Besides, I'm not certain I would want to support Allende. It's all over the newspapers what he's doing to break apart the country."

By the time she'd finished speaking, everybody else in the room had stopped talking and was looking at the two of them.

"Don't you read the newspapers?" she asked Mario after a moment of silence, not having understood why the room had suddenly grown so quiet.

"Since when have you started reading the newspapers?" Angel asked Consuelo as they walked back to the *pensión*.

"You can see all the headlines at the newspaper stands," she said, thinking that to have been obvious enough.

"Oh," Angel replied. "So, you haven't actually started reading the newspapers — just the headlines."

"Why do you care, anyway?" Consuelo asked, Angel's tone having upset her. "You heard Mario — apparently it's all lies."

Angel suddenly stood in Consuelo's way, making her stop with him. "Whether you choose to believe it or not, there is a war going on in this country and it's only going to get worse. There are a lot of rich and powerful people who don't like that Allende was elected and they will stop at nothing to change that."

"You and Mario and all your other new friends take yourselves far too seriously," Consuelo replied, disregarding Angel.

"The highest-ranking officer in the military is assassinated and they're still trying to sort out what happened almost three years later?" Angel continued. "There are only two options here — either the police are hugely incompetent or it's a conspiracy at the highest level."

"Schneider was killed during a robbery. Even I know that," Consuelo said, certain of at least that because that was what she'd heard her father tell another man in church. "Do you know how paranoid you sound?"

"Schneider was the strongest supporter of the idea of democracy within the army and there's no way he would have allowed the military to meddle in politics like they've started doing now," Angel replied. "General Prats is just barely hanging on."

"You're being ridiculous. What does the army have to do with anything?" Consuelo responded. "You and your friends are just trying to make yourselves out to feel superior to the rest of us."

"You have no idea how much I wish you were right," Angel said after a brief moment, and Consuelo had not expected that.

The following weekend, Angel didn't even ask Consuelo to go out with him again and Consuelo wasn't certain if it was to spare her from the humiliation she'd experienced the week before, or to save him from any further embarrassment that she might cause.

"There are a lot of different groups you can join at the university," Angel said before he left that night. "You should try to find one you're interested in."

"You don't have to worry about me, Angel. I'm perfectly capable of taking care of myself," Consuelo replied, perhaps trying to convince more herself of that than Angel.

"Well, then I'll see you later," he said before leaving.

From her window, Consuelo watched Angel walk off down the street. He seemed so intensely focussed as he headed off in the dark, and it was clear to Consuelo that at long last, he had found his place.

As the weeks went by, watching Angel disappear into the night from her bedroom window had become a new routine for Consuelo, and she was even able to find an odd sense of comfort in the certainty of that. One weekend, though, she was surprised to find a woman waiting for Angel. Consuelo had thought nothing of it when she'd first noticed the woman down on the street that evening — the woman simply seemed to be waiting for somebody. But then Angel stepped out of the *pensión,* crossed the street and went directly to her. Consuelo watched, absolutely stunned, as Angel put his arm around the woman while the two of them walked off together.

Consuelo couldn't stop replaying that scene over and over again in her mind when she tried to get to sleep that night. She decided that it was good that Angel had finally gotten himself a girlfriend because she wouldn't have to worry about his feelings for her any more. But yet, a disturbing sense of uneasiness still lingered in her mind — a sense that she had lost part of herself in the moment when Angel had put his arm around that woman. What she was left with was the darkness around her, and the sounds from outside that made their way in through the walls and the windows. It only upset her more when she heard Angel return to his room later that night, knowing that in all those hours he was gone, she'd been unable to get him out of her mind.

12.

Consuelo walked home from university alone that after-noon, just as she had for the past few months. She'd waited for Angel at the end of each day for a couple of weeks after classes had begun, but more often than not he would be late. Consuelo had soon started to feel that she was an inconvenience to him and so one day she simply decided to head home without waiting for him — it wasn't as though she didn't know the way or that it was especially late, after all. Consuelo had been working on her homework on the balcony by her door overlooking the inside patio for well over an hour before Angel appeared. She heard somebody rushing down the courtyard and looked down, hoping that it would be him — hoping that she'd finally caught his attention. When Angel saw her, he stopped abruptly.

"I was frantic looking for you," he said, clearly upset.

"I've been here for quite some time," Consuelo said, unaf-fected by his tone.

"You could at least have had the decency to tell me you weren't going to wait for me."

"How could I? You weren't there for me to tell you," she responded.

"I was just a few minutes late," Angel said.

"Because you were busy talking to your more important friends and you lost track of the time again," Consuelo quickly added.

"When did I ever say that — ?" he asked, clearly surprised by her words.

Angel started walking up the stairs towards her then.

"You don't actually have to say it for me to see it," she told him, quickly collecting her books and standing up, anxious to move away before he reached her.

"That's not true at all," Angel said emphatically. "You're very important to me."

"Save your lies for your girlfriend," Consuelo blurted out before returning to her room and shutting the door behind her; she knew that if she provided Angel the opportunity to respond she would be unable to stop him from convincing her that he was right, and she didn't want that to happen.

When Consuelo walked home after her classes were done, she varied her route. The streets in the neighbourhood were filled with many little shops and cafés, and each day she was able to discover something new and interesting. This new routine lifted Consuelo's spirits; it allowed her to entertain herself without needing to rely on anybody else and kept her away from the *pensión* for a few hours so that she would not find herself missing Angel. Though she didn't have much money, every now and then she was able to buy something small to divert herself, like some barrettes for her hair or some earrings, and other things that made her feel pretty.

Normally, Consuelo would stay away from the expensive clothing boutiques that dotted the streets, knowing that she would never be able to afford anything in them. One afternoon, though, she decided to go into one to try on some new dresses; just for a few moments, at least, she could pretend to be somebody else.

When she was looking through one of the dress racks, she caught a fleeting glance of a person through the mirror in front of her — somebody who walked past the store on the street outside. Though she only caught a brief glimpse of the person as he walked by, Consuelo could have sworn it was Felix and so she quickly turned around to look out the front window of the shop, but the person was gone. She rushed out of the store and saw a man crossing the street farther down the block, then turn a corner and walk out of sight. The man walked with the same stride as Felix and carried his body exactly the same way, but Consuelo was certain that her mind must have been playing tricks on her because Felix was hundreds of miles away in Chillán. But regardless, her curiosity got the better of her and led her to follow the man who had disappeared. She crossed the street and turned the corner, but from there he was nowhere to be seen.

After that, Consuelo started taking that same route home from school every day, the idea that the man could possibly be Felix having come to consume her. She was soon unable to think of anything other than Felix, fixated on the idea of meeting up with him again and re-establishing their relationship. Each day, Consuelo would stand and wait at the corner where the man had turned, at the exact same time, but nobody even resembling Felix ever walked by. After a week, Consuelo finally accepted that it must have been nothing more than wishful thinking that had caused her to think it could have been him in the first place. That day, she decided to head to one of the sidewalk cafés instead, to enjoy a cup of coffee while she reviewed her class notes.

The strangest feeling made her look up from her notebook just as she finished her coffee, and in that moment she found herself looking straight at Felix.

"I thought it was you," he said.

"Felix — ?" she managed to utter after a moment of being caught at a complete loss for words. "What are you doing here?"

"It's nice to see you, too, Consuelo," he said, smiling, giving her a far more light-hearted expression than she had ever recalled seeing from him before.

"It's just that I thought you were in Chillán," Consuelo clarified, not wanting Felix to think that she wasn't pleased to see him.

"Going to technical school was my father's idea. It really wasn't the place for me."

"So you decided to move here?"

"This is where all the opportunities are," he said.

"You have a job here?" Consuelo asked.

"Yeah," he said after hesitating for a moment.

"That's wonderful," Consuelo said.

"Were you planning on meeting somebody?" Felix asked then, looking at the empty chair beside her.

"No, I was just going over some of my class notes," she replied.

"Is it all right if I join you?" he asked.

"Of course," Consuelo responded, quickly clearing off her books from the table and tucking them back into her bag.

Felix smiled as he sat down and Consuelo found herself falling for him over again, every bad memory she had ever had of him suddenly fading; the only thing that mattered to her in that moment was that he was there beside her now.

"*Señora* Carmen told me you've been coming in late a lot these past few weeks," Angel said.

"Why does it matter to her what I do?" Consuelo asked.

"She's worried about you."

"Well, you can tell her I'm fine."

When Consuelo arrived at the *pensión* that night, Angel had been waiting for her. He was leaning up against the wall by her door, smoking a cigarette. It was well after midnight and everything around them was quiet and dark.

After their few brief words, Consuelo unlocked her door and turned on the lights to her room as she stepped in.

"I know you've been skipping your classes," Angel said, following her into her room.

"You want me to believe that you have perfect attendance?" Consuelo responded as she set down her things on the bed.

"We both know it's more than just every now and then," he said.

Consuelo turned to him, curious. "How would you know that?"

"I have friends in your classes," he told her.

"You're spying on me — ?" Consuelo asked, stunned.

"Call it what you want," he replied. "It doesn't change the fact that you haven't been going to your classes for some time now and you're coming home late every night."

"What I do is none of your business," Consuelo said, upset that Angel of all people would be reprimanding her.

"You're wrong about that — I promised your father that I would look after you," Angel said.

"That's what you call spending all your time with your new friends and completely ignoring me?"

"You keep saying that, but you're the one who pushed away from me," he said.

"Your new friends clearly don't like me," Consuelo responded.

"Your problem isn't that my friends don't like you or that I don't spend enough time with you; your problem is that you can't stand not being the centre of attention every single moment of the day," Angel said, stunning Consuelo with the harshness of his tone. "If that's what you're looking for, you should have stayed at home with your father, because I guarantee you with absolute certainty that nobody is ever going to come even close to treating you the way he does. That's what you don't like about my friends — that they don't indulge you or lie to you to make you feel better about yourself."

Consuelo walked over to the door and held it open for Angel. "If you're done scolding me, you can leave."

"It's not a good time to be making questionable decisions," Angel said after a moment of silence, not making any effort to move. "With the military action on the *Moneda* the other week, its just not safe."

"The military action on the *Moneda* — ? You mean the tanks that drove by the Presidential Palace?"

Angel looked at Consuelo briefly, clearly disappointed with her.

"You need to take me seriously when I tell you that you should trust nobody — certainly not in this city and not now," he allowed after a moment.

"Well, if that's what you're concerned about, there's no need for you to worry because I haven't met anybody new," Consuelo said with the greatest sense of satisfaction. "Felix has moved here and we've started seeing each other again."

"Felix... " Angel said, smiling glibly as he absorbed Consuelo's words. "Well, then I guess you're right. I guess there is no reason for me to worry now that you're back in his capable hands, is there?"

After a moment of silence, Angel turned and headed out to his room next door. Consuelo peeked around the corner after him, curious to see if he would give away anything with his movements, but there was nothing at all abrupt or rushed in his actions. Angel quietly shut his bedroom door as though nothing about their exchange had upset him, and that lack of response disappointed Consuelo. Though she did not want Angel to interfere with her life, she did wish he was more attentive to her like he had been when they were in high school. As it was, this was the first time she had seen him in weeks, and it was only because Carmen had said something to him and not because he'd actually noticed anything himself.

Angel could do what he wanted, though, Consuelo thought to herself. He and his friends could keep believing themselves to be doing important work when they met at night and talked about politics, because Consuelo had Felix now. Felix had been so caring and tender towards her since they had met up again at that café, and he was able to make her feel special just by the way he looked at her. He never talked down to her or tried to make her feel that he was better than her, not like Angel. Angel was free to walk away from her — with Felix back in her life, what Angel did was not of significance to her anymore.

For the first few weeks after she had started seeing Felix again, Consuelo continued going to her classes, but soon started to find it all too overwhelming. She was unable to keep up with her homework without any free time in the evenings or weekends, and whenever she missed a class to spend the time with Felix instead, she would find herself falling even more behind. With the next set of exams coming up in only a few weeks, Consuelo had come to the conclusion that the only way she would be able to pass any of them was if she dedicated all her time to attending class and studying — but the last thing she wanted to do was to stop seeing Felix, if only temporarily. She decided to stop going to her classes instead, because she knew she was going to fail regardless.

She knew that her parents would be disappointed in her, but they were far away.

A heavy winter rain set in the following night. All day it had looked as though the weather could not make up its mind — whether to allow the sun to shine or instead to cover everything up with clouds. As night emerged from the evening, though, dark clouds rolled in and brought with them an unbearable humidity that enveloped Consuelo when she had walked home earlier. The rain now finally provided some relief from the smothering sensation that lingered even indoors, but it came with such a loud ferocity that it kept Consuelo from falling asleep. She got up and watched the rain from her window for a while. It beat down hard on everything, washing away all the dust and dirt that had found its way onto the streets and the buildings and taking it down through the gutters. The rain continued for a long time that night, much longer than usual, and Consuelo was left wondering what it could be that it was trying so desperately to wash away.

Consuelo thought of Angel again just moments before finally managing to fall asleep. She wondered if the rain had kept him awake also, but then became upset with herself for continuing to think of him, still.

13.

"What's wrong?" Felix asked, Consuelo's sudden unease having been clear for him to see.

"Nothing."

"Is it those women back there?"

Consuelo had hoped Felix wouldn't have noticed her looking back at them earlier. Something about one of them had struck her when the two walked into the restaurant just as Consuelo and Felix were starting their meals, but she wasn't sure why. It occurred to Consuelo only after glancing back at the woman a few times that she was the one Angel had met out on the street that one night.

"So, Angel finally has himself a girlfriend..." Felix said, smirking to himself.

Felix had been so insistent about knowing why she'd kept looking back at the two women that Consuelo had found herself with no other choice but to tell him why. The conversation, though, made Consuelo uncomfortable. Even though both Angel and Felix always made fun of the other to her, she especially did not like talking about Angel to Felix, regardless of the reason.

"Which one is she?" Felix asked, looking back at the women.

"She's the one sitting on the far side, with the long hair."

Consuelo watched Felix look at the woman for what she felt to be an inappropriately long time. It wasn't just how long he looked at her that made Consuelo feel uneasy, it was also the way he looked at her — it was very deliberate, as though he wanted to take in every part of her. When Felix finally turned back to Consuelo, he quickly moved in to caress her face.

"She's not nearly as beautiful as you," he said, taking away all her concern in that moment.

"He's a drug dealer — that's how he makes his money," Angel told Consuelo a few days later. "Actually, he'll do pretty much anything for cash."

"Who are you talking about?"

"Your boyfriend," Angel replied.

Angel had been waiting inside Consuelo's room when she returned that evening. When she went to unlock the door, she noticed it was already open. At first she thought she must have forgotten to lock it that morning when she'd left, but then she saw Angel inside sitting on her window sill when she walked in and turned on the lights.

"Why are you so jealous of Felix that you have to stoop to lies?" Consuelo asked, not believing one word of what Angel had said. "He does odd jobs for people, but that doesn't make him a criminal."

"I just don't want you to complain to me later that I didn't warn you," Angel continued after a brief moment. "He sells mainly to rich kids. They have a lot of money to spend and Felix is more than happy to find ways for them to part with it."

"Is that why you're here? To try to convince me that Felix is a bad person?"

"No, I didn't come here to try to convince you of anything — I know you better than that," Angel responded. "I came here to tell you that I called your father to tell him you're not doing well in school and that he should come take you back home."

"You what — ?" Consuelo asked, completely stunned.

"He'll be here next week," Angel continued, unaffected by Consuelo's reaction. "I told him to make sure you're back home by Independence Day."

"You just can't stand to see me happy without you, can you — ?"

"I'm not going to argue with you, because you're never going to believe anything I say anyway. But for what it's worth, this has nothing to do with Felix," Angel replied. "I don't like the way September's started and I think it's best for both of us to leave."

"This martyr routine of yours is really starting to bore me," Consuelo said, needing Angel to believe that whatever he did would not affect her.

"I'm leaving," Angel said suddenly, seemingly out of nowhere.

"What do you mean, you're leaving — ?" Consuelo asked.

"I'm going to lay low for a while, under the radar," he replied.

"You're kidding, right — ?" Consuelo asked, certain that it should have been a joke, but sensing that it wasn't. "Where are you planning on going?" she continued after a moment.

"I think it's best for both of us if I don't tell you," Angel said.

"You come in here with all this drama and secrecy, and still expect me to believe this has nothing to do with Felix?" she said.

How Angel responded to her next, though, completely surprised Consuelo because he'd never done anything like that before: he walked up to her and very softly and tenderly touched her cheek. There was not the slightest hesitation or doubt in his movement, and the touch of his hand against her face was so honest and so unlike the way she felt when Felix touched her. Consuelo had to pull away from him, overwhelmed by the sensation he'd left her with.

"If you ever dared let yourself truly compare the love I feel for you against whatever it is that Felix feels, you would know the truth," he finally said. "But there's more to life than love, Consuelo, and measured up against so many other things that are happening right now, love really is a very small thing."

Angel looked at her for another moment, with only silence between them, and then started to leave.

"I'm never going to forgive you!" Consuelo told him as he walked away from her.

Angel stopped and seemed to hesitate, but only briefly.

He turned back to look at Consuelo, still very calm. "But I will forgive you. And when you need me the most, I will be there without question. Never doubt that."

Angel's voice was very soft and his tone peaceful, and with his words he managed to make Consuelo feel so very ashamed of herself for the way she'd spoken to him. She did not say anything more to try to stop him, because she knew he'd already left her.

Consuelo looked out her window to the street below after Angel had left. She watched him step out onto the sidewalk and cross the street. Just then, he stopped and looked back up at her window — she quickly stepped away, not wanting to give him any more of herself, not even one more memory to be left with.

Consuelo noticed Angel's bedroom door was open as she headed out to see Felix the next day. She couldn't stop herself from taking a look inside, thinking it possible that Angel had changed his mind and had come back. When she looked into the room, though, *Señora* Carmen was cleaning it up. Carmen looked up when she noticed Consuelo in the doorway.

"Sometimes they can be so serious at this age," *Señora* Carmen said, more to herself than to Consuelo, shaking her head in disbelief. "They think they can change the world," she continued as she stripped the bed.

Consuelo gave Carmen a small smile in acknowledgement, not having anything to say in response.

"Your father phoned last night while you were out," Carmen added almost as an after-thought. "He said he'll be here next weekend."

"I see," Consuelo managed to respond, trying her best not to show *Señora* Carmen any of her dread.

Consuelo didn't even want to begin to think about what would be in store for her when her father arrived. She knew that Angel had told him that she wasn't doing well in her classes, but didn't know if he'd told him anything more. Consuelo wondered if she could even begin to explain to her father what had happened without disappointing him, but then it occurred to her that she could lay the blame on Angel himself. Angel had left her alone, after all, spending his free time with his new friends and his girlfriend instead of accompanying Consuelo and helping her with her homework. The story was not entirely the truth, but it was not entirely a lie, either.

"He's not here," Felix's roommate told her at the door.

"Oh," Consuelo replied, not having expected that because Felix had told her he'd be there all day.

"You can wait for him if you want," the roommate offered after an awkward moment of silence. "I just don't know how long he'll be."

Consuelo stepped into the darkened apartment and watched Felix's roommate head off down the hallway and disappear into his own bedroom, closing the door behind him. Consuelo looked around hesitantly for a moment, uncertain what to do. She looked into the living room — there were clothes and magazines strewn about and the coffee table was littered with dirty dishes and half-empty pop bottles. She then looked down the hallway again, in the direction Felix's roommate had gone.

After lingering in the entryway for a while, Consuelo decided to go to Felix's bedroom and wait for him there. His room was just as messy as the living room, though, and Consuelo had to clear a spot for herself on the bed to have somewhere to sit. After a few minutes, she decided to lie down and close her eyes for a bit as she waited, her sleep the night before having been so restless that it had left her still groggy and tired when she woke that morning.

The next thing Consuelo realized, a bright light suddenly flashed into her face in the darkness. She recoiled and brought her hand up to block the light from her eyes. She was completely disoriented and unable to see anything, but then she heard Felix laugh and she remembered where she was. His bedroom was so dark now that she realized she must have fallen asleep.

"Felix! What are you doing?"

Felix pulled his flashlight to the side, pointing it away from her face.

"Relax," he replied. "I was just having some fun."

"Being scared awake like that isn't my idea of fun," Consuelo said, sitting up. "What time is it, anyway?"

"It's just after seven."

"I thought you said you were going to be here this afternoon," Consuelo said.

"Something came up."

"Like what?"

"Just some stuff," Felix replied evasively. "Trust me, you wouldn't want me to bore you with the details."

Later that evening, Consuelo noticed that Felix was still behaving oddly, continuing to evade her questions and for some reason insisting on steering the conversation back to Angel at every opportunity. Felix had taken her out to a nice restaurant to make up for how upset he'd made her — or at least that was what he'd told her — but his behaviour now only served to make her even more suspicious of his motivation.

"Why are you asking so many questions about Angel?" Consuelo finally asked. "Since when does it matter to you what he does?"

"I'm just expressing an interest in your life," Felix answered, but the words seemed unnatural coming from him.

"Angel isn't my life," Consuelo clarified.

"I thought you were good friends," Felix tried to explain.

Consuelo looked at Felix, trying to see what she was missing, but his expression gave away nothing.

After a moment, Consuelo noticed Felix glance at a man who had walked into the restaurant only a few minutes earlier and taken a seat at the bar. Felix looked back at Consuelo and smiled at her when he noticed her staring at him.

"Did you want another drink?" he asked as he got up from the table.

"No, I'm fine."

"I'm going to get myself a refill," he said, quickly finishing off his half-full glass of whiskey and heading over to the bar.

Normally, Consuelo wouldn't have given his departure a second thought, but this time she kept replaying what Angel had said the night before, and so she watched Felix from the corner of her eye, careful to make sure that neither he nor the other man at the bar noticed her looking at them. The man handed Felix a small envelope as the bartender refilled

Felix's drink, and Felix exchanged the envelope for another one he had in his pocket. Felix then grabbed his refilled drink and returned to the table. He smiled at Consuelo as he sat down, but that only served to compound Consuelo's feeling of humiliation.

Consuelo studied the butterflies for the longest time in her bedroom later that night. She had stripped off her clothes in the bathroom when she'd returned to the *pensión* earlier and had scrubbed her whole body with a wet washcloth, feeling the desperate need to wash away the sensation of Felix from her body. She had left his bed that evening after they'd had sex feeling smothered by him — not physically, but somehow just with his presence — and she had needed to get away from him. The sensation of her clean skin refreshed her and cleared away the thickness that had come to wrap itself around her.

Consuelo looked down at the butterfly case as she sat on her bed, the small pins carefully holding open the shimmering wings of them, one after another, all three so perfectly in line. The case was one of the few things she'd taken with her to Santiago, along with her clothes and some books. Her mother had picked it off the night table beside Consuelo's bed when she was helping her pack and placed it with her pile of things to take.

"You don't think it will break?" Consuelo had asked her mother.

"Eventually," her mother had responded cryptically; she'd sounded like she'd wanted to say something more, but had left it at that.

Consuelo slowly traced the outline of each butterfly with her finger. She hoped she would be able to put herself in that memory again, of when she and Angel had run through the fields as children, with the butterflies fluttering all around them. But all she was able to find were small fragments of moments; nothing that could take her mind away from the lonely room she sat in now.

14.

The room was cold and dark, and in it Consuelo was unable to stop shivering. At least there she was alone, though, away from the soldiers who walked through the corridors and all the sounds that seeped in around the edges of the door. There were echoes of footsteps, sometimes steady and calm, and other times more rushed and frantic; the sound of doors opening and closing, the slamming reverberating and giving away just how long and empty the corridors were; and there were loud, pain-filled screams.

It took her eyes some time to adjust to the darkness of the room after she was locked in it. After sensing she was alone in the room, she felt along the walls searching for a light switch, but when she finally found one, it did not work. There were no windows or any other source of light in the room, but after her eyes had adjusted to the dark, the light that streamed under the door from the corridor was soon sufficient for her to make out the shapes of the objects around her. The room itself was small, the size of a storage closet. She noticed something farther off at the back wall as she surveyed the room and walked over to get a better sense of what it was. When she felt it with her hands, she realized it was a small wooden bench and she sat on it to rest. After a while, she decided to lie down on it, curling up to find some warmth.

Consuelo was unable to stop herself from drifting in and out of sleep, waking every now and then with each sound, regardless of how soft it was, and then falling back to sleep in the moments when quiet managed to seep into the room again. Consuelo lost all track of time with this sleep pattern and she did not know if she'd been there for days, or possibly just hours or even minutes. Regardless, she found sleeping when she could manage it to be more of a comfort than staying awake and alert in her surroundings, waiting without knowing what was in store for her.

In the moments that she was awake, Consuelo found herself replaying the last few days over and over again in her mind, going through every single word that Angel and Felix had said to her, not knowing exactly what it was that she had missed, yet knowing that she had missed something.

Three days after Angel had left, Consuelo went out for *almuerzo* with Felix — there was nothing unusual in that, except that she had had more to drink than she normally would. It was rare that she would ever drink more than a glass of wine during a meal, but Felix kept pouring her more even though she never fully finished her glass, and so she wasn't certain exactly how much she had drunk. Felix had behaved oddly again that day, but Consuelo had started to expect that from him and so it did not stand out to her that afternoon. He kept glancing at his watch as if he were waiting for somebody, but nobody else showed up — at least nobody that led him away from their table.

Just as they were finishing their meals, the waiters started going from table to table, asking everybody to leave because they were closing up early.

"The radios are reporting a curfew's been declared," the waiter who came up to their table explained.

Consuelo tried to understand the waiter, but even though she had heard what he'd said, his words made little sense to her in that moment — all she understood was that they had to leave, but she wasn't certain why. She tried to stand up, following Felix's lead, but stumbled, and Felix had to steady her; it was only then that she'd realized how drunk she was.

Out on the street, everything was surprisingly quiet, far quieter than it normally would be on a weekday afternoon.

"I should take you back to your place," Felix told her, taking her hand and starting to lead her down the street without giving her the chance to respond or even to regain a sense of herself.

Felix walked Consuelo only as far as the street corner by the *pensión*, though, and not all the way to the door — but the fact that he had even bothered to walk her that far was unusual because normally he would have just called a taxi for her. Consuelo turned back to look at Felix when he abruptly stopped at the corner and lit a cigarette.

"Go on home," he said when he noticed her hesitate, and after another moment Consuelo did exactly that.

When Consuelo reached the front door she stopped and looked back at Felix again, but he was looking off in another direction. By then, though, the light sensation of all the wine she'd drunk that afternoon had turned into a heaviness and she felt an overwhelming need to sleep, and so she went inside without giving Felix another thought.

"Hurry up and get inside," *Señora* Carmen said, rushing up and closing the door behind Consuelo.

Consuelo looked at Carmen curiously, not understanding her urgency.

"Don't you realize what's happening?" Carmen asked. "Never mind now — just hurry up and stay put in your room," she continued without giving Consuelo a moment to respond.

Consuelo wasn't certain how long she'd slept that afternoon. She remembered that it was still light outside when she'd returned to her room because she had to close the drapes to shut the brightness out. She'd lain down on her bed to try to clear her head and it seemed to her that in the very next moment it was suddenly pitch black and a bright light was flashed in her face. The contrast of the light and darkness surrounding it was extreme, and Consuelo immediately moved her face away from the light.

"I thought you were going home," Consuelo said, still groggy from the wine.

The light moved then, following her face.

"Felix! Cut it out!"

"Consuelo Hernandez?" a man's voice asked harshly; it was not a voice that she recognized.

Consuelo quickly sat up. She put her hand up to block the light to try to make out who was there with her in the darkness, but a gloved hand pushed her back down in her bed.

"Who are you?" she asked.

"Consuelo Hernandez — is that your name?" the man asked again.

"Felix, this isn't funny! Quit fooling around!"

Consuelo started to push herself up again, but was stopped by the knife-point of a bayonet against her neck and she froze.

"Look — I don't have much here, but there's some money in the top drawer of the dresser and you can take that,"

Consuelo said, still not understanding what was happening around her.

The knife-point edged in a little deeper against her neck — not enough to hurt her yet, but the message was clear.

"Just tell me your name."

Consuelo absorbed the man's eerie tone, then looked down at the knife-point against her neck — its blade was flawless, without even the slightest warp or stain, and it perfectly reflected the light that fell against it. The reflection flickered briefly as the blade moved slightly, giving away that it was held by human hands.

"My name is Consuelo Hernandez," she finally said, having grown too tired and too frightened to continue with her protests.

Without any warning, she was grabbed from her bed and pulled out of the room. It was then that she realized it wasn't just one man in the room with her, but several, all dressed in military uniforms. As they dragged her out onto the court-yard balcony, Consuelo noticed other soldiers rummaging through Angel's old room.

"Where's your friend?" one of the soldiers asked as he stepped out of Angel's room.

Consuelo was still so shocked by everything around her that she couldn't even begin to formulate a response to his question.

"What's the matter with you, are you deaf?" the soldier asked, his tone more irate now than it had been before.

"I don't know where Angel is," she managed to respond, having determined that it would be far better to say anything than nothing at all. "He packed up and left a few days ago. He didn't say where he was going."

The soldier just looked at Consuelo then, perhaps trying to assess if she was lying or not. "Get her out of here," he finally instructed the others around them.

One of the soldiers behind her motioned with his bayonet for Consuelo to go down the stairs and she did exactly that without another word or motion of protest, sensing that doing what she was told was in her best interest. She walked carefully down the stairs and through the courtyard out to the front entrance, knowing full well that the rifles in the hands of all the soldiers around her could be quickly pointed in her direction if she were to do anything else.

Consuelo caught a glimpse of *Señora* Carmen from the entryway just before she was shoved out onto the street. The door to Carmen's suite was the tiniest bit ajar and Consuelo could see Carmen peeking out through the crack, their eyes meeting for a fraction of a second.

"Why are you stopping?" the soldier behind Consuelo asked.

The door to *Señora* Carmen's room very quietly shut in that moment, just as Consuelo herself was pushed out the front entry.

Out on the street, Consuelo was ushered onto the back of a waiting military truck and a soldier followed in behind her, motioning for her to sit. From her seat in the truck, Consuelo looked out to the front of the *pensión* where some soldiers started to gather and she saw Felix walking up towards them — it was very dark, but even though she couldn't make out his face clearly, she was certain it was him by the way he moved and a sudden wave of relief came over her.

"Felix!" she called out.

Felix turned around and looked directly at her, but only in a casual manner. He clearly made eye contact with her, but offered nothing more.

"Felix!" Consuelo called out again. "It's me, Consuelo."

She was sure that he must not have realized she was the one calling out to him, because if he had, he most certainly would have tried to help her. Felix's gaze remained the same, though — matter-of-fact and completely devoid of any emotion, as if she were still nobody he recognized. Felix finished smoking his cigarette and then dropped the butt onto the ground and crushed it with his feet.

The soldier beside Consuelo in the truck pulled her back down to her seat and motioned for her to be quiet. The back doors of the truck were closed right after that, creating a loud clanging sound. Consuelo could still see Felix through the back window — he was laughing with some of the soldiers in front of the *pensión*. Consuelo still couldn't understand how it was possible for him not to have seen or heard her when she'd called out to him so loudly. She continued to watch him, hoping he would glance over in her direction and see her, but he never did.

When the truck finally started to drive off down the road, Consuelo glanced at the soldier sitting beside her. She wanted to ask him where they were taking her and why, but was stopped by his stern expression. She decided instead to try to make out whatever landmarks they passed along the streets, but the effort was completely futile on her part because the night was pitch black and she could see nothing through it.

15.

"You're free to go home whenever you'd like," the soldier told her in a matter-of-fact tone as he sat across from her.

"I am?" Consuelo asked, finding it hard to believe — the offer seemed so out of context and she'd come to understand that she should take nothing at face value where she was.

Earlier, when the guards had gotten her from the dark room where she'd been left waiting, she asked if she could go to the bathroom, needing desperately to go there after having been left in the room for so long. When they took her to the bathroom, Consuelo didn't give a second thought to pushing the stall door closed behind her, even as one of the guards held it open, assuming that he would let it shut — he did not, though, and instead became visibly upset with her.

"Am I not allowed some privacy?" Consuelo asked, thinking the request to be only reasonable.

The guard just looked at her for a moment without responding and then suddenly grabbed her by the throat with such a force that he almost pulled her off the ground.

Consuelo was overcome with immense pain, and by a sudden inability to breathe. She felt an overwhelming pressure building up in her head, a sensation she found utterly unbearable. Then, the guard abruptly let her go, leaving Consuelo to stare at him in shock.

"If you want to go to the bathroom, go now," he said.

The guard stepped a bit back then, but still kept the door open; it was for this reason that she doubted her interpretation of the soldier's offer to her now in the interrogation room.

"Yes — you are free to leave as soon as you tell us where your friend is," the soldier responded to her question now as he sat in front of her.

"What friend?"

"Angel Torres."

"Oh," she replied, understanding then that that was the reason she wouldn't actually be able to leave.

"You're not going to try to convince me that you don't know him, are you?" the soldier asked.

"No, of course I know him. He's my cousin."

"All right, then," he said, clearly waiting for her to tell him more.

"But I don't know where he is," she continued. "All I know is that he left a few days ago."

Consuelo watched as the soldier's lip curled down tightly — and yet, he offered no other reaction to her, not a word or any other movement.

"Really, that's all I know," Consuelo said, feeling the need to assure him that she was telling the truth, finding the length of his silence while waiting for him to respond or react in some way simply too unnerving. When she finished speaking, though, the silence continued.

Only after what seemed to Consuelo to be an eternity of silence did the soldier finally react, suddenly getting up from his chair and walking around to her. He stopped just behind her, beyond where she could see but close enough for her to sense him. She did not dare look back, though, in spite of how much she wanted to do just that, knowing that would be a mistake.

Suddenly, Consuelo felt a gloved finger touch her face.

"Do you know how beautiful you are?" the soldier asked, though his words did not seem like a compliment to Consuelo.

"Really, quite like a work of art, actually," he continued after a moment. "Which is why it sickens me so much to hear you lie."

Consuelo suddenly felt a strike against the side of her head with such force that it knocked her right off her chair. The pain that welled over her in that moment was so sudden and sharp, and the ringing in her ears so loud, that she barely noticed her impact against the concrete floor below her; suddenly, she found herself sprawled there, unable to distinguish which way was up because the room around her was spinning.

With her hands on the floor in front of her, Consuelo was finally able to steady herself. When the dizziness started to settle, she noticed something across from her in a darkened shadow in the corner of the room — something she hadn't noticed before. Consuelo had been seated so quickly on the metal chair in the middle of the room when she was first brought in and the light in front of her had been so bright that she hadn't been able to see anything beyond what was closest to her. Sprawled on the floor now, Consuelo focused her gaze on the object in front of her and realized a woman was curled up against the wall, her clothes half-ripped off and clearly having already been beaten. The woman looked up only briefly but, even though her look was quick and her face badly bruised, Consuelo immediately recognized her as Angel's girlfriend.

"I see the two of you had the chance to get your stories straight," Consuelo heard the soldier say over the loud ringing in her ears. "And here Felix told me you two didn't know each other."

"Felix." That was the only word that stuck in Consuelo's mind.

"You're not ever going to find Angel because he knew better than to tell anybody where he was going," Consuelo heard the woman in the corner blurt out with a force that seemed incongruous with her physical state. "But even if we did know, we'd never tell you because we would never betray him like that."

The woman's words immediately caught Consuelo. She did not know what stunned her the most about them — the fact that the woman dared to speak so wilfully, clearly knowing full well what she was risking, or that she really did love Angel, and in a most selfless way.

The woman's words were met with the eeriest of silences, though, one that Consuelo found almost painful because of the anticipation of what was about to happen, which was sure to be terrible. But instead, the soldier started to clap, loudly and deliberately.

"That was quite a performance," he said. "But none of that is actually true — isn't that right, Consuelo?"

Consuelo's mind quickly moved back to the thought of Felix again, replaying the memory of when she'd last saw him when she was in the military truck. She remembered not understanding how it was possible for him not to have recognized her even when she'd called to him so loudly and it occurred to her only then, as she lay on the cold, hard floor, that maybe it wasn't that he hadn't recognized her, but rather that he simply hadn't cared.

"You know, Consuelo, it isn't nice of you to not answer when I've asked you a question."

"I don't know what you're talking about," Consuelo responded, barely audible even though she'd intended for the words to come out louder.

"I can't hear you," the soldier replied. "I might hear you better if you were standing up instead of lying on the ground."

Consuelo was not anxious to move, but feared what would happen to her next if she defied him again. From somewhere deep inside, she managed to find the strength to lift herself up, first sitting up and then finally standing. It took her a moment to stabilize herself, the room having started to spin again the moment she lifted her head off the ground, but when the spinning stopped she looked straight at the soldier.

"I said, I don't know what you're talking about," Consuelo repeated, this time far more insolent and curt in her tone, surprising even herself when she heard the words come out of her mouth.

Almost immediately, she stumbled back and was unable to stop herself, her head hitting hard against the back wall. She crumpled to the ground and a sharp, burning pain grew inside her again. The memory of what had happened revealed itself to her only then — more like something that she'd seen than actually experienced herself — of the soldier striking her and her head jerking back as her feet stumbled to follow. From the ground by the wall, she could see the soldier's boots stepping towards her, the light reflecting off them with each step he took and for a brief moment Consuelo found herself completely mesmerized by the light that bounced back.

The soldier crouched when he reached her. He then grabbed her by the chin and forced her that way back up onto her feet again.

"Why don't you tell your little friend why she's here, Consuelo?" he said looking straight at her, his expression beyond rage.

"I don't know why she's here," Consuelo replied automatically, having finally come to the conclusion that there was nothing she could do or say that would stop the process of humiliation that was planned for her; all that was left for her now was to speak the truth.

"Sure you do — it's because you offered her to us," the soldier said. "Every time you told that boyfriend of yours something, you might as well have been telling it to me directly. The girlfriend was a gem, because we would never have known about her by ourselves. That alone was worth all the money we paid him."

Consuelo's mind went back to that afternoon when she saw Angel's girlfriend at the restaurant and how she'd pointed her out to Felix. Consuelo had wanted him to reassure her that she was the more attractive of the two, and Felix had played her so artfully that she had completely missed what he had in fact been doing.

The soldier finally took his hand away from under her chin and walked away, smirking to himself. He seemed to understand that Consuelo knew he was telling the truth.

Suddenly, an immense wave of nausea came over Consuelo. She managed to bend over just a bit by the wall before throwing up, a strong burning sensation ripping through her. She wiped her mouth before standing up and looking right back at the soldier again, needing to do that.

Before the soldier even had a second to react, though, the door to the room opened and three more soldiers walked in. With the bright light that suddenly came in from the corridor, Consuelo was unable to make out anything beyond their shapes, and when the door closed behind them, all she could see were their outlines in the dark. The soldier already in the room attentively stood up, giving away that he was not the most important among them.

"Colonel," the soldier said, offering a salute.

"Who are these two?" the one he'd addressed as Colonel asked, referring to Consuelo and Angel's girlfriend.

"Dissident Angel Torres' cousin and his girlfriend, sir," the soldier replied. "We haven't been able to locate Torres yet. He's from your home town, though, and so that's why I thought you would want to be briefed.

"That's his cousin?" the Colonel asked, hesitating briefly before speaking.

"Yes," the soldier replied.

After what seemed to Consuelo to be a profoundly long silence without even the smallest of sounds or movements coming from anybody in the room, the Colonel stepped in closer to her. He was so close to her that she was able to clearly make out every feature of his face — his clear green eyes and his pale skin that was lighter even than hers. If the two of them were from the same town, she had never seen him before.

"What are you doing with her?" the Colonel asked, his question clearly intended for the soldier behind him even though he did not turn back to look at him.

"She's useless for information," the soldier replied. "But she is a very beautiful woman and there's no need for that to go to waste," he continued.

Consuelo saw the Colonel close his eyes when silence had returned again. It seemed to Consuelo as though he were trying to absorb something in his mind, as if he had needed that moment of pure thought. When he opened his eyes again a few seconds later, his expression was the same — fixed and steady — and he still did not glance away even once from Consuelo.

"Let's leave the Colonel alone," the soldier told the other two soldiers, starting to lead them out.

"No," the Colonel said firmly. "Stay," he continued, the word definitely an order.

The three soldiers stopped and looked back at the Colonel. Consuelo noticed the Colonel take hold of something at his side and she looked down to see him bringing up a gun. He brought it right up in front of her face, his expression heavy. Consuelo looked at the gun — it was virtually identical to her father's, like the one she'd seen him carry in his side holster all her life, and perhaps it was for that reason that the gun in front of her now did not frighten her. She closed her eyes, not wanting to see any more; she knew it would be better like that. As she heard the gun cock, she thought that at least there would be grace in not having to remember.

Then, the loud sound of the gun being shot burst through her ears, and that shot was followed by two more.

Even with that, though, Consuelo did not feel the pain of the bullets go through her and could still feel herself to be. She opened her eyes, curious to know if she was shot dead and that was what it felt like. When she looked down at her body, though, she could see no gunshot wounds and no blood. The Colonel was by the woman in the corner, giving her his jacket to cover herself. Consuelo looked all around the room, trying to make sense of what had just happened, and that was when she noticed the three soldiers slumped down on the ground, a bullet wound in each of their heads, oozing with blood — all dead.

The Colonel turned back to Consuelo after helping the other woman up and offered her his hand. Consuelo looked at it curiously, still not understanding what had just happened.

"Why are you doing this?" she asked.

What came next, though, was a thick moment of silence, and only after that had passed did the man answer: "Because. I have a daughter," he said, pausing between the words, as if for some reason they were too heavy for him to say all at once.

"Should I know you?" it occurred to Consuelo to ask, struck by just how comfortable she felt in his presence, not feeling any threat in him at all.

"We have to hurry," the Colonel said, motioning for her hand. "We only have a bit of time."

Consuelo looked at his hand again and took it. His hand felt warm and it grasped hers with a sturdiness that assured her with all certainty that he would protect her; she did not know why, but she trusted that.

16.

Consuelo studied her bruised and swollen face in the mirror. She caught sight of her eyes — her clear hazel eyes — and the way they stared back at her made her uneasy.

She had decided to stay seated in the bathroom that morning, having grown tired of rushing back there from her bed every time she had to throw up. The nurses had told her to try and drink water, but that only served to make her feel worse. In the bathroom, she was finally able to find some peace away from all the strangers around her in the hospital; alone, at least she could cry.

Earlier, when she was still asleep, she had felt a shadow standing over her and the feeling had disturbed her. She heard whispers and muffled voices and had tried to make sense of what was being said, but the meaning eluded her. Suddenly, a flurry of movement rushed in, making the air stir and flutter in her ear, urging her to wake up. In her mind, she desperately tried to follow the instruction she was given, but her body refused to accept her will. And then, everything quickly grew quiet and still again, and she knew without needing to be told that the shadow was gone. When she finally did wake, Consuelo was unable to shake an overwhelmingly disturbing feeling of loss.

"Where am I?" Consuelo had asked the nurse who came into her room shortly after she'd woken.

"You're in the hospital, dear," the nurse responded. "Don't you remember coming here?"

Consuelo thought for a moment and tried to remember just how she'd arrived there, but could find only fragments of memories flickering in her mind, images that came in briefly before disappearing and not staying with her long enough for her to be able to piece any of them together.

"No, I don't remember," Consuelo told the nurse. "Just that somebody took my hand and urged me to wake up."

"Maybe it's the Colonel you're thinking of — he's the one who brought you and your friend here."

"The Colonel — ?" Consuelo repeated, her memory suddenly rushing back. "Where did he go?"

"He said he was going to contact your parents."

"Does he even know who I am?" Consuelo asked, wondering how he could have known who she was or how to reach her parents.

"He said your name is Consuelo Hernandez. Is that your name?"

Consuelo looked at the nurse, the way in which she'd phrased her question having put her on edge.

"It's all right to be confused, dear," the nurse said, responding to Consuelo's sudden hesitancy. "How you and your friend were attacked in the street like that, and for what — ?" she continued, shaking her head in disbelief.

"I was attacked in the street?"

"It's a good thing the Colonel came across you when he did," the nurse said, nodding her head. "Otherwise, who knows what could have happened."

"But, I thought I was in the stadium?" Consuelo asked.

"Not in it, dear — just outside it on the street. The stadium is where they're rounding up all the criminals," the nurse clarified. "The Colonel said you might be confused," she added after a moment.

"Oh," Consuelo said, understanding even less with that explanation.

"Don't worry, you're safe now," the nurse tried to reassure her. "And I'm certain your parents will be here just as soon as they possibly can."

Consuelo soon realized that the Colonel must have told the hospital that story to explain the state they were in when he brought them there; perhaps telling the truth was too dangerous even for him.

"Is the Colonel coming back?" Consuelo asked.

"He said he was," the nurse responded before continuing with her work, checking Consuelo's temperature and examining the states of her many cuts and bruises.

Consuelo glanced around the room to orient herself within her new surroundings. She noticed something on the table beside her and was stunned to see, when she leaned in to get a better look, that it was her butterfly case. She took it in her hands and looked up at the nurse, not understanding how it could have gotten there.

"A young man left it for you when he came by yesterday," the nurse explained. "You were still asleep, so he didn't stay long."

"Angel?"

"I think that's what your friend called him."

"My friend — ?"

"Yes, the one who was brought in with you," the nurse clarified. "She was doing much better than you and so he came by to take her home."

Consuelo stared at the nurse, suddenly understanding the dream that she'd had. Angel was the shadow that had stood over her while she'd slept and then left, leaving Consuelo there alone.

Only after the nurse had left the room did Consuelo dare look back at the case again; she felt so many different emotions all at the same time, overwhelming her, and she suddenly started to cry. One of the tears that streamed down her face caught her lip and she was able to taste the salt of it.

Maria Soledad cooled Consuelo's forehead with a wet washcloth. The only sound in the room was that of the splashing water echoing as her mother dipped the cloth into the water basin — there were no words to be said.

Manuel had stayed with them in the room only for a short time, the peace and quiet it contained seeming to have made him uneasy. He gave himself away with the weight of his footsteps as he paced back and forth, with the brief, lost stares with which he'd absorbed all the cuts and bruises on his daughter's face, and then finally with the way he'd abruptly left the room.

He eventually returned a while later, but this time stood in the doorway holding the door part-way open.

"Maria Soledad," he called out quietly, seeming not to want to disturb Consuelo even though she was quite clearly awake.

Only when Maria Soledad turned back to look at Manuel did Consuelo notice another man standing in the corridor a bit behind her father. Consuelo wasn't able to make out the other man very well because her father's shadow blocked out all the light around him, but she knew it was the Colonel.

Maria Soledad briefly turned back to look at Consuelo and Consuelo noticed her mother pause hesitantly for a second, seeming to be caught off-guard. Consuelo couldn't ever recall a moment when she'd seen her mother react like that before, and so for that reason found her mother's behaviour curious. Manuel motioned for Maria Soledad to go to him, and Maria Soledad did, but only after closing her eyes for another moment and taking a deep breath. By the time she finally reached the door, though, her mother seemed to have recovered her sense of self because she looked directly at the two men as she spoke, giving away to neither of them the hesitancy she'd allowed Consuelo to see only moments earlier. Although Consuelo was not able to hear any part of their conversation, she found herself unable to stop looking at her mother — the way Maria Soledad stood and the way she moved her head and nodded as the men spoke seemed very confident, and yet there was something forced and unnatural about it.

Suddenly, the conversation stopped and Manuel looked back at Consuelo again with a sad and heavy look. The Colonel stepped back farther into the hallway after another moment and then even his shadow disappeared from Consuelo's sight. She could hear his footsteps grow distant as he walked off down the corridor, the sound finally fading out completely; after that, Consuelo heard nothing more.

"It isn't safe for you to be here any more," Manuel told Consuelo, breaking the silence that had come to engulf the room. "They're focusing their search on Angel even more now that he killed those three soldiers and God only knows what they'll do to you if they find you again."

"What soldiers?" Consuelo asked, but then remembered that there had been three other soldiers with her in the interrogation room, along with the Colonel.

"Colonel Ross said you'd probably still be confused about everything that happened over the last few days," Manuel responded before Consuelo had the chance to say anything more. "As long as they're still looking for Angel, you won't be safe."

"But I don't know where Angel is," Consuelo told her father.

"That doesn't matter to them — the only thing that does is that Angel has humiliated them."

"But you're a police officer — you can protect me," Consuelo said.

Manuel looked at Consuelo, but offered no response. It seemed to Consuelo that she'd caught him off-guard with her words.

"I need to be absolutely certain that nothing like this ever happens to you again," Manuel finally allowed. "The Colonel is making arrangements for you to leave the country."

"Leave the country — ?" she asked, stunned.

"It's the only way we can be certain that you'll be absolutely safe."

"Where am I going?" Consuelo asked after a moment, realizing that it had already been decided.

"To Canada," Manuel hold her.

"I don't even know where that is," Consuelo said after fully absorbing her father's words.

"It'll just be for a little while, just until the country gets back to normal. You'll be back before you even know it."

"Is Canada close?" Consuelo asked, sensing that it wasn't.

Manuel only looked at his daughter then, but provided no actual response.

"Canada is far away on the other side of the ocean," her mother said after a moment, daring to tell her daughter the truth.

Maria Soledad returned to her seat beside Consuelo's bed then, and took her daughter's hand. Manuel watched the two of them for a while, then left the room once more; the silence that had returned again seeming to have unnerved him.

"What am I going to do?" Consuelo asked her mother quietly after her father had left.

"You're going to do what everybody else in this world does," Maria Soledad responded. "You're going to survive, because that is what you have to do."

"But I'm not as strong as you are," Consuelo said.

"Surviving has nothing to with strength," Maria Soledad replied in a soft tone. "All you need to do is just keep waking up every morning and let the day carry you."

Consuelo continued looking at her mother, but did not say anything more; she was disappointed by the patience of her words. Just in that moment, though, it occurred to Consuelo that her mother must have known the Colonel from before — the two of them seemed to be about the same age, and if he actually was from their town, it would have been impossible for them not to have known each other, at least by sight.

"Was he your friend?" Consuelo dared ask her mother then, needing to know. "Is that why he's doing all this?"

Maria Soledad looked at her daughter, clearly understanding the question even with all the words she left out.

"My father and brothers all worked for the Ross family at one time or another," she said. "The last of their family left town about four years ago. There was a lot of talk that Allende would take away their land if he became president, and so they sold it before the elections. But most of the family had already moved away by then."

"Did Angel's father work for them?" Consuelo asked.

"Yes — right up until the day the last of them left."

"Angel was here," Consuelo told her mother, even though she sensed it wouldn't be a surprise to her. "He brought me the butterflies," she continued, motioning to the case on the night table beside her.

Maria Soledad glanced over at the butterflies, but didn't say a thing.

"He wasn't the one who killed those soldiers," Consuelo said.

"I know," her mother replied.

Consuelo studied her mother's expression, struck by how easily she'd accepted her words.

"Should I know him?" she asked.

Maria Soledad started to straighten her daughter's hair, seeming to find some kind of comfort in doing that. "Sometimes there are questions in life you don't really want to know the answers to," she finally responded, but only after a long moment of silence.

Consuelo continued looking at her mother, trying to understand what she'd meant with her vague response. She wondered if she should push her for more of an explanation, but by the stolidness of Maria Soledad's expression, Consuelo knew that her mother would tell her nothing more.

It was almost three months later when she received the letter, just shortly after she'd moved into her new apartment in Winnipeg. The handwriting in which her name was written immediately caught her attention, and when she looked at the return address, it was from Angel's old room at the *pensión*.

Inside the envelope was a newspaper article and a very brief note: *"Consuelo — You know it wasn't me. You know it didn't happen this way. I know you know that."*

Consuelo went on to read the article, which had a picture of Colonel Ross in the corner — it was about his murder. He was alone in his house the day after Consuelo had left the country and had been ambushed there, his assassin having tried to make it look like a suicide by using his own gun against him.

The article continued: *"The known rebel leader, Angel Torres, already implicated in the cold-blooded murder of three other soldiers only weeks ago, is the prime suspect and an aggressive manhunt is already under way for him. Colonel Patrick Ross is survived by his parents, his siblings, and his nieces and nephews. He had no wife or children."*

Consuelo reread the last sentence again: *"He had no wife or children."*

That evening before going to bed, Consuelo looked at herself in the mirror in the bathroom, examining every detail of her face. By then, her scars had faded to the point that she might not have found them if she didn't know they were there. She was far thinner now than she'd ever been before and her face looked as if it had been chiselled and sculpted. And then there were her eyes. She knew that face, daring to recognize it completely as it stared back at her — in that moment, she knew who it was.

Then, just as she'd done every other night since arriving in that cold, cold place, she curled up into a tiny ball in her bed and cried until all she could feel was the burning sensation in her eyes. When she finally fell asleep, she remembered nothing more.

17.

She wasn't surprised when the doctor told her. She had felt sick for some time and had not managed to get better. When she'd first arrived in Canada, her body seemed to settle down a bit, with the sudden nausea that would come over her every now and then having diminished in frequency. When she moved into her new apartment, though, she started to feel worse all over again. Consuelo had initially thought it was all the time she'd spent cleaning the apartment that first day that had made her sick again, as she'd spent hours dusting and vacuuming everything she could, and even washing down the walls. She was so excited to finally have her own private space and to be able to leave the hotel where she'd stayed with the others who had arrived from Chile that she hadn't realized just how long she'd spent cleaning until she started to feel faint again. Later that night, the nausea and fatigue grew much worse than she'd ever experienced before, and so she'd decided to go see the doctor the next day.

It wasn't the news that she was pregnant that surprised Consuelo, but rather that she was pregnant with twins.

"How could that be?" she asked the woman who was sent in to translate for her.

"It's just something that can happen randomly," the woman replied after talking to the doctor briefly in English. "Sometimes there's a family history."

Consuelo thought of the last time she'd seen her aunts, when they came to help her mother prepare her farewell party just before she'd left for Santiago. She remembered watching them as they'd scurried about, fascinated by how truly identical they were — not only in the way they looked, but also in the way they moved their bodies and how they held themselves. Consuelo had always found them to be so identical that her mother constantly had to keep clarifying to her which one was which.

"How can you tell them apart?" Consuelo had finally asked her mother that afternoon when she'd found her carrying some plates to the dining room.

Consuelo had wondered what it was that she'd missed, because her mother was always able to distinguish the two of them without ever hesitating

"Maria Mercedes is the shy one and Maria Lucinda is the strong one," her mother had answered Consuelo's question without giving it a second thought.

Consuelo had been surprised by her mother's response, having expected her to point out some physical characteristic that Consuelo hadn't noticed — that one was slightly shorter or that perhaps one had slightly different colour eyes — but not that the difference was in their personalities.

That evening after she returned home from the doctor's office, Consuelo studied her body in the bathroom, trying to imagine the twins she was carrying. She thought it odd that there could be life growing inside her, something that was so much a part of her and yet so separate from her at the same time. She wondered if she would be able to distinguish the two of them the way her mother could distinguish her sisters — beyond their appearances, down to something in their characters or maybe even to the essence of their beings. She wondered if they know she was their mother. Would they understand that they had lived within her, floated inside her protected from everything else in the world from the very moment they'd begun to form? Would this be a knowledge they were simply born with?

"Will you be able to inform the father?"

Consuelo hadn't expected the social worker to ask about the father, but in hindsight she knew she shouldn't have been surprised. The doctor had told her the social worker would help her prepare herself, given that her pregnancy was giving her some concern and he considered it to be high-risk. Consuelo should have known that sooner or later somebody would bring up the matter of the father.

"We might be able to work on bringing him here if he's in the same situation you were in," the social worker continued.

"He's dead," Consuelo heard herself respond, the idea entering her mind almost in the very moment she spoke the words. "He went missing a few days before the coup and nobody's heard from him since," she added after a moment, needing the social worker to believe her and not ask anything more about him.

Consuelo found herself replaying the social worker's words over and over again in her mind for days and weeks after, still unsettled by them. The sudden possibility they presented to her made her feel ashamed of what she found herself hoping; she wondered what the power was that Felix held over her even then that he could make her want him so irrationally, still. Even in the hospital in Santiago, she had been so conflicted about him — wanting in moments to tell her father everything that he had done, not doubting for one moment the vengeance that Manuel would exact, but at the same time not being able to bear the thought of living the rest of her life without the possibility of ever seeing him again.

Now, alone in her apartment, Consuelo found herself wanting him just as desperately as she had the very first time she'd met him. She started to doubt all that she already knew was the truth — maybe she'd misunderstood what had happened in the interrogation room, or perhaps lying to her and making her doubt Felix had been part of the torture. Or, if it had been the truth, it could have been Felix, himself, who had been somehow deceived by the military — he could have come to realize only afterwards just what had actually happened, after Consuelo had been taken and not returned. He could have been frantically looking for her even in that very moment, needing desperately to find her and explain.

Consuelo thought writing him a letter could do her no harm, regardless of what actually was the truth; she could send the letter to his parents' home, and certainly they would forward it to him. If Consuelo was wrong about Felix, there was nothing more he could do to her from so far away, but the hope that she wasn't wrong was far more powerful than any other thought that ran through her mind.

Early the next morning, she headed out to drop off the letter in the mailbox. It was the first time she'd stepped outside of the apartment block in several weeks — after her last visit to the doctor, she'd been instructed to rest as much as possible and to avoid standing or walking for any prolonged length of time. A woman had been assigned to her to do all her household chores and her grocery shopping, so that Consuelo wouldn't have any need to leave the apartment for any reason or exert any physical effort. Consuelo had considered giving Felix's letter to that woman to mail, like she did all her other letters, but she needed to know with absolute certainty that the letter had made it safely to the mailbox and so instead had decided to drop it off herself. Consuelo had thought the short walk to the post office surely would not be too hard on her and that perhaps the sun and fresh air would actually do her some good.

"You were in the hotel, too," the man who stopped to hold the front door open for Consuelo said in perfect Spanish.

The man had been walking in just as Consuelo had started to head out. Consuelo hadn't thought much of his gesture, nor had she even really looked at him, and so the fact that he spoke to her in perfect Spanish surprised her. When she looked back at him, though, she did remember him — he had arrived at the hotel a few days before she'd moved out.

"Did you just move in?" the man asked.

"No," Consuelo replied, immensely relieved that she was finally able to speak to somebody in Spanish after struggling for so long to get by with her broken English. "It's just that I've been told to stay inside and rest as much as possible because of the pregnancy."

"Where are my manners — ?" the man continued, holding out his hand for her to shake. "My name is Pedro Salazar. I'm from Temuco."

"I'm Consuelo Hernandez," she replied in turn. "I was a university student in Santiago before all of this," she added, not interested in telling him anything else.

"The students were hit very hard," Pedro said, nodding as if he understood. "In a place as big as that, I'm sure there's a rat hiding in every corner, no matter how much you try to avoid them."

Consuelo just nodded then, uncertain what her words would give away to him if she said anything more and needing for him not to know.

"Where are you going?" he asked after a moment. "Maybe I can help you."

"I'm just going to the post office to mail a letter."

"But the post office is several blocks away," he said, visibly stunned by Consuelo's words. "It's very cold outside and with the wind it's barely tolerable in the best of circumstances."

"I'm sure I'll be fine."

"At the very least, let me accompany you," he offered.

"No, really, I — " Consuelo started to respond, but then had to stop abruptly when a sudden, sharp pain came over her, as though something were grabbing and twisting her from the inside. She found it impossible to keep her balance and grabbed on to Pedro's arm to stop herself from falling over.

"Didn't I tell you to stay inside and rest?" the doctor asked as he walked into Consuelo's hospital room. "What would have happened to you if your neighbour hadn't been there to help you?"

Consuelo wasn't interested in defending herself to the doctor, though, as by then the pain had grown to the point where that was all she could think of. Regardless, though, she understood from the doctor's tone that he wasn't actually looking for a response.

"We're going to have to get you into the operating room to get those babies out as soon as possible," the doctor told her after briefly examining her. "The nurses are going to start preparing you shortly."

Consuelo looked up at the doctor, not understanding why he would be taking the babies out when she wasn't even seven months pregnant.

"How can that be good for the babies?" Consuelo asked, managing to find the strength to give voice to her thoughts.

"We need to get them out of you before your body kills them or they kill you. Do you understand that?" the doctor replied. "And no — none of this is very good for your babies."

After the doctor left her room, Consuelo noticed her coat hanging up inside the tiny side closet, the door having been left slightly ajar after one of the nurses had helped her get changed. She could see the tip of her letter to Felix sticking out of the top of her pocket, still waiting where she had left it, and its presence now only made her feel profoundly humiliated. What could ever have possessed her, she wondered to herself. Felix had only ever taken away things from her — all the love that she had ever had in the world and even her home, and he had left her desolate.

Consuelo let the nurses and orderlies prepare her without asking any more questions, knowing that the only thing that mattered in that moment were her babies inside her fighting for their lives. The only words that came from Consuelo after that were in response to the questions she was asked: *Did she feel all right? Was she comfortable? Count backwards. Count backwards...*

18.

They were such tiny little girls, more like dolls than real people. She wanted so much to touch them, but was scared that she would break them, even just by softly caressing them with one finger. Each one of them was wrapped tightly within a small blanket and placed in her own individual bed, both covered with transparent cases with all sorts of tubing going in and coming out. Mainly, Consuelo just sat and stared at them, uncertain what more she could do.

"Have you picked any names yet?" the nurse asked Consuelo when she took her in a wheelchair to see the girls after she'd awoken from her sleep.

"I haven't thought of any I like," Consuelo responded, though the truth was that she hadn't spent even one moment thinking of names — everything about her pregnancy had been so overwhelming to her that the thought of having two tiny babies in the end had never seemed fully real.

"Maybe seeing them will give you some ideas," the nurse suggested as she wheeled Consuelo into their room.

Consuelo hadn't expected to see her two babies encased the way they were, or for them to be so tiny. They were both far smaller than any baby she'd ever seen before, their arms only slightly bigger than her fingers.

"Is there something wrong with them?" Consuelo asked the nurse as she glanced around the room, seeing all the different machines connected to her daughters' bodies.

Consuelo noticed the nurse hesitate and glance back at another nurse in the room before responding; "The doctor will be here in a few minutes and he'll be able to answer all your questions."

Consuelo sat in the maternity ward for hours later that day, looking at all the healthy newborn babies. She watched the visitors that came by — mainly fathers and grandparents, she assumed by the look of them — and watching them made her think of her own parents. She wondered if she should tell them about the girls or if there was even any point to that if neither of them survived, as the doctor had told her could very well happen.

The doctor's words had been slow and deliberate when he spoke to her that morning, as if he wanted to be absolutely certain that she understood him. Consuelo didn't know what to feel and perhaps her expression gave that away; everything around her had been more like a dream since she had woken from the operation, with her head still cloudy and her reactions delayed.

"We can arrange for a priest to come," the doctor offered, still seeming unsure how to interpret Consuelo's reaction even after she'd assured him that she understood.

"Why a priest?" Consuelo asked, confused.

"To baptize your daughters," the doctor explained. "You are Catholic, aren't you?" he asked, flipping through the papers in her file.

"Yes," Consuelo answered. "I guess that would be a good idea,"

She had thought about telling her parents before, long before she'd given birth, as she'd received letter after letter in the mail from her father. Each of his letters arrived so closely one after the other that Consuelo had found it difficult to keep up with her responses, managing to reply only after every third or fourth one, and even then having so little to say to him; mainly, she would just confirm that she'd received his letters and that she was well. In his letters, her father would write to her about every happening in their small town — about who had been to church that Sunday and what had been announced, about all the crops that were in harvest and even the meals that her mother had prepared; he summarized all the things that had happened and that were planned to happen, always avoiding talking about feelings other than to say that he missed her.

Every time Consuelo had thought about writing back to her father about her pregnancy, though, she would soon quickly discount the idea without understanding specifically why. For some reason, it seemed to her that putting her life down in words as it was happening to her would somehow suddenly make it real and inescapable. But now, without her having written even one word, her daughters had still come to be; and yet, the reality of it wasn't at all like she'd feared. Instead, she was fascinated by the life that had been created within her; to put that into words now and to share that with her father, she thought, would certainly not spoil a thing.

"There you are," Consuelo heard Pedro call out from behind her.

Consuelo turned and saw him walking towards her with a small bunch of flowers.

"The nurses told me I might find you here," he said. "Which ones are yours?" he continued after a moment, looking into the nursery.

"Mine aren't there," Consuelo replied. "They're in a different area because they were born prematurely."

"I see," he said, seeming uncertain what more to say. "They asked me at the nursing station if you'd picked out any names for your girls yet," he added after a moment, as the thought seemed to come to his mind.

"Why would they have asked you that?" Consuelo asked, finding it odd that they would have asked that of a virtual stranger.

"I told them I was your friend," Pedro explained apologetically. "They didn't know that we only just met."

"Oh."

"Have you picked out names for them?" he asked.

"I haven't come up with any I like."

"Maybe there's a name in your family that might be nice — perhaps your mother or grandmother's name?" Pedro suggested.

"No," Consuelo replied, resolute in at least that.

Pedro just stared at Consuelo then, seeming to be at a loss for what more to say. Consuelo was far too tired to worry about how to move the conversation along, but her glancing at the flowers in Pedro's hands seemed to do that all on its own.

"Where are my manners?" Pedro asked quickly, more to himself than to Consuelo, and then held out the flowers for her to take. "I brought these for you."

As Consuelo took them, she realized that Pedro was the only person in her whole life who had ever given her flowers.

"I can take you back to your room if you want," Pedro offered. "That way, I can put the flowers in some water."

Consuelo stared at the flowers in the vase for a while later, after Pedro had left them on the table beside her uneaten meal.

"Well, I guess I should head back home," Pedro said, glancing at his watch.

Consuelo gave him a small smile in response, grateful that he had come by to visit and that he had diverted her mind for a while.

"You were going to send a letter — " Pedro said after suddenly stopping at the door. "Did you want me to mail it for you?"

Consuelo glanced at her closet door, which was now closed.

"No, not that letter," she responded. "It's old news now," she continued, hoping that would serve as enough of an explanation for Pedro.

"Right," Pedro said quickly.

"Maybe you can come back tomorrow, so that I can finish a letter to my parents," Consuelo said.

"I'd be more than happy to do that," Pedro responded, smiling. "Until tomorrow," he confirmed and then headed off on his way.

When the nurse woke her in the middle of the night, it felt to Consuelo as though it had been only moments after she'd finally managed to fall asleep; she had tossed and turned for quite some time, unable to find a comfortable position and distracted by all the unfamiliar sounds around her.

"It's one of your girls," the nurse said as she shook Consuelo awake. "We've already called for a priest."

"What time is it?" Consuelo asked as she looked around in the darkness, far too groggy with sleep to make sense of what was happening.

"The doctor doesn't think she's going to make it through the night," the nurse told her, and only then did it become clear to Consuelo why she'd been woken.

Consuelo softly caressed her daughter, having been assured by the nurse that her touch would feel good to her daughter and that she would find it comforting knowing that her mother was there.

Consuelo looked at her other daughter beside her then. When she was first taken to the nursery that night she was told that her other daughter was not at risk — she was a strong girl even though she didn't look it and was doing much better than the doctor had expected. Looking at her now, Consuelo tried to see if she could tell the difference between her and her other daughter, certain there had to be something, but she found that neither of them was bigger than the other and that they were identical in at least every way that she could physically discern. She wondered if the difference was beyond something she could see, to the core of their personalities, just like what distinguished her twin aunts from one another.

It happened so quickly after that: the sound of the machine by her sick daughter abruptly changed its rhythm, without even the slightest warning. The rhythm turned erratic for a quick moment and then blurted out a continuous sound, mirroring the change in her daughter's body — the way in which her stomach had moved up and down as she'd breathed and then suddenly stopping. Consuelo watched the nurse turn one of the knobs on the machine, lowering the volume of it until it was no longer audible.

"What is this child to be named before God?" the priest asked her, having arrived only a few moments later to perform the baptism.

"Angela," Consuelo responded, knowing with certainty that if there was a heaven, her daughter would be there, spared of all the things in life Consuelo would not be able to protect her from. Perhaps Angela had understood that, Consuelo thought to herself — perhaps that was why she'd made that choice.

Consuelo was unable to sleep afterwards. Angela had been taken from the room shortly after her death and baptism, and her other daughter was suddenly left without the only companion she'd known from the very moment she'd begun to form. Consuelo sat by her for hours after, even as night turned to morning, not daring to touch her and not wanting to interrupt her sleep, but just wanting to accompany her, to be sure. That desire surprised Consuelo; she felt a stronger sense of attachment to both her daughters than she had ever thought possible, and she needed to be certain that her other daughter would be all right on her own.

When Pedro arrived later that afternoon, Consuelo had already finished her letter to her parents, writing them about the life she had given to her two daughters, and the death of one. With her words, she felt she had made both of their lives real and known, and unchangeable — needing that to be so — and it was only after she finished her letter early that morning that she had finally allowed herself to fall asleep.

"They told me about your little girl," Pedro said. "I'm so sorry to hear that."

Consuelo offered Pedro a small smile in response, not wanting to say one word about it, knowing that if she did she would cry and she did not want Pedro to see her like that. For some reason, she needed him to think she was stronger than she actually felt herself to be.

"Can you help me with this?" Consuelo asked after a moment, motioning to some forms beside her. "They want me to fill these out, but I can only make out some of the words."

"I was an English teacher in Chile," Pedro told Consuelo as he took the forms and started to read them.

"The nurse said they're birth certificates," Consuelo said.

Pedro nodded. He took off his jacket and sat down on the chair by Consuelo's bed, setting the papers up on the table in front of him. He took out a pen from his shirt pocket and started writing.

"The mother's name is Consuelo Hernandez — is that correct?" he asked without looking up from the form.

"Yes."

"And the father's name — ?"

Consuelo looked at Pedro then, caught unprepared.

"The father's name?" Pedro asked again, looking up at Consuelo this time, perhaps thinking that she hadn't heard him before.

"The social worker told me that I didn't have to name a father," Consuelo finally responded. "She said it would be easier for me that way, because he's missing and nobody knows if he's dead or alive."

"And your daughters' names?" Pedro continued, seeming to have accepted her response without question, to Consuelo's immense relief.

"Angela and Pilar," Consuelo said.

"Angela and Pilar Hernandez — very pretty names," Pedro commented.

"Yes, they are," Consuelo agreed.

19.

"I discussed the possibility of this with you before," the doctor told Consuelo, his tone clearly giving away his frustration with her.

"But I've never seen this happen to anybody before," Consuelo responded. "How could everything be all right?"

"It's more normal than you think," the doctor replied. "She may have some trouble getting her muscles to do all the things she wants them to do, but she's perfectly normal in every other way — her intelligence won't be affected, nor will her overall health. She has a relatively mild case of cerebral palsy, and that's it. She might need to use a brace when she starts to walk because her left leg could be stiff and shaky, but that really will most likely be the worst of it."

"Why is this happening?"

"It's hard to say exactly how it could have happened. It might have happened very early on in the development stages, before you even knew you were pregnant."

"But her whole body shook uncontrollably," Consuelo explained again, certain the doctor must not have understood her fully the first time, given how calm he was.

"It's part of the illness, but it can be controlled with medication," he told her.

Her daughter was peaceful in her arms in that moment, her calmness seeming to want to reassure Consuelo and soothe her, as if Pilar herself somehow understood what was happening to her and yet was unconcerned.

Consuelo didn't know what time it was when she awoke that day. She had stayed in the hospital the entire night before waiting for news about her daughter and when she was finally able to take her daughter back home in the morning, all she wanted to do was sleep. When Consuelo woke, the only light she could see was what streamed in from behind the drapes — it was so faint that she thought it must still have been day, but just barely. Her daughter stirred beside her, too, and Consuelo suspected that likely the same thing had woken them both, but she wasn't certain exactly what. Just then, she heard some knocking at the front door, the sound muffled by the distance. When she managed to reach the front entry, though — not rushed in any way and certainly not with the intention of actually opening it, but rather merely curious to see who was there — the knocking had stopped. She looked out the peep-hole and saw Pedro walking away from the door. He opened the side stairwell door and disappeared, and after that all Consuelo could see was the emptiness of the corridor before her.

"It's good to see that your daughter's better now," Pedro told Consuelo a few days later when she bumped into him as she went down to check her mail, finding the usual letter from her father there. "I went by your apartment a few days ago, but I guess you hadn't returned yet," he continued.

Consuelo couldn't help but stare at the scars on Pedro's face as he spoke. She'd noticed them for the first time that night when they'd waited for word about her daughter in the hospital, and she had wondered then why she hadn't seen them before. Perhaps it had been the brightness of the light in the waiting room and the way it had glared down on them so harshly that made them so obvious that night, she had thought. The scars themselves clearly weren't new, but there were so many of them running down his cheek and his neck; even as faded as they were, they gave away so much about Pedro.

Pedro had stood up abruptly in the hospital waiting room after Consuelo had first noticed his scars. She'd wondered if he had felt her looking at them and that that had caused him to walk away. She watched him for a while as he walked down the corridor, his pace consciously slowed as though he wanted to extend his walk for as long as possible. He would glance at people that walked by him every now and then, but mainly he just stared off into the distance, seeming to be looking at nothing at all — it seemed to Consuelo that he preferred that.

Everything had happened so suddenly earlier that night, catching Consuelo utterly unprepared: Pilar's tiny body started to convulse furiously, her eyes darting around and her whole body becoming limp, without any conscious movements coming from her but only violent shudders and twists of her muscles. And then, as quickly as it had started, the convulsing suddenly stopped. Her daughter opened her eyes again and smiled at Consuelo, seeming not to have been affected at all by what had just happened, or even to be aware of it. It was then that Consuelo's panic set in, making her anxious to do something, but without knowing exactly what that should be.

Consuelo rushed up to Pedro's apartment with her daughter, frantic and desperate, the only idea that had occurred to her. Pedro's suggestion to call a taxi to take them to the hospital seemed simple and obvious, but only when he spoke it.

They had been waiting at the hospital for several hours after Pilar had been whisked away and it was already close to morning when Pedro returned from one of his walks with two coffees.

"I wouldn't go so far as to actually call this coffee myself," he told her, holding out one of the cups for her to take. "But it might help wake you a bit."

"It was very nice of you to have brought us down here, but you really don't have to stay and wait with me," Consuelo said.

Perhaps it was the way in which her words had come out — she'd only meant that Pedro shouldn't feel obliged to wait with her when he was clearly so tired. By the reaction on Pedro's face, though, it became apparent to her that she'd disappointed him with her words. He seemed not to want to let on to her, but he had already given himself away.

"Are you sure you'll be fine?" he asked after a moment of hesitation.

"You've already done so much for us and there really isn't anything more either of us can do now except wait," Consuelo replied, this time choosing her words more carefully. "I'm sure you have plans for tomorrow and you won't be any good if you don't get some rest."

Pedro briefly looked down at his coffee on the table beside him before grabbing his jacket and leaving.

Consuelo thought about Pedro again the following day when she returned from the hospital with her daughter. She wondered if stopping by his apartment would be the appropriate thing to do, so that he could know that they had returned safely, but she was so tired from the whole ordeal and her sleepless night that she decided instead to head directly to her apartment — she could thank him some other time.

"If you aren't doing anything right now, why don't you stop by for some tea?" Pedro asked Consuelo as they both stood by the mailboxes in the apartment lobby now.

"I certainly wouldn't want you to go to any trouble," Consuelo responded after a moment of hesitation, knowing it would be ungrateful of her to turn down his offer even though that was exactly what she wanted to do.

"Nonsense," Pedro replied quickly. "Tea isn't any trouble at all. I was already going to make myself a pot, so I'll just add some more water."

She felt awkward then, because of the way Pedro looked at her and her daughter, and the tone in which he'd spoken. Consuelo wondered about his motivation and all the things that were left unsaid but were so obviously there, almost as visible to her now as his scars had become.

"Do you like milk or sugar in your tea?" he asked her from the kitchen.

"Just some sugar, please," she responded.

As Pedro moved about in the kitchen, Consuelo glanced at all the things he kept out in his living room. Some photographs on a side table caught her attention: the first one of an older couple, and then one of a woman with a young boy.

"Have I shown you a picture of my son?" Pedro asked as he walked out from the kitchen with two cups of tea and a plate of shortbread cookies.

"I didn't know you had a son," Consuelo remarked.

"He's three years old now," Pedro told her, taking one of the photographs and handing it to Consuelo for her to have a better look. "His name's Pedrito."

"Where is he?" she asked, curious.

"With his mother back in Chile," Pedro replied. He then anticipated her next question before Consuelo even asked it: "She was too scared to come here with me and it was too dangerous for me to stay there."

"Is that her?" Consuelo asked, motioning to one of the photographs.

Pedro nodded in response, but said nothing more.

His wife was a pretty woman, simple in her style, and Consuelo stared at her image for a while, mesmerized by everything it revealed about Pedro.

"When everything returns to normal in Chile, we'll both be able to go back home to our families," Pedro said.

Consuelo looked at Pedro, wondering how much of what he'd just said he actually believed. Perhaps he said it more to convince himself, she thought.

After a moment, Consuelo took a sip of her tea — it was far stronger than she would have liked and left a harsh, bitter taste in her mouth. She glanced up at Pedro and he smiled at her, seeming not to have noticed her reaction to the tea.

Pilar suddenly started to become like a heavy weight in her arms and Consuelo shifted her around.

"Were the doctors able to tell you anything?" Pedro asked, looking at Pilar.

Though Consuelo was relieved to have something to be able to talk to Pedro about that didn't leave her feeling so awkward, talking about her daughter's illness only served to make her frustrated all over again.

"Your doctor is right — it is quite common," Pedro tried to reassure her after she'd explained to him as much as she'd understood the doctor tell her.

"He said she'll have problems walking and that she might even need to use a brace on her leg," Consuelo added, flustered by the calmness of Pedro's words.

"Well, thank goodness it's just that and nothing worse."

Consuelo smiled flatly at Pedro, not finding his words remotely comforting, yet knowing that was how he'd meant them. She took another sip of her tea, certain it would still taste bitter but hoping that drinking it would help move the time along quicker. She found it interesting that the more she made herself drink the tea, the more she grew used to its strong flavour; after a while, it didn't seem even slightly bitter to her any more.

"More tea?" Pedro asked as he looked at her empty cup.

He didn't even wait for her response, though, before walking to the kitchen and returning with the pot to pour her some more.

Consuelo quickly put her hand over her empty cup, stopping Pedro in mid-motion.

"I really should be getting back to my apartment," she explained when he looked up at her curiously. "I was planning on writing a letter to my father," she added, Pedro clearly needing more of an explanation by the way he continued looking at her.

"Of course," Pedro said, setting the pot down. "You have other things to do."

Consuelo studied Pedro's expression — it seemed to her that he wanted to say something more but wasn't certain if he should. Finally, she started to get up from the table.

"Consuelo — " Pedro said, touching her hand with his; his hand was warm and moist, and the softness of his touch made her very uneasy.

After a moment of silence, Consuelo looked up at Pedro, waiting for him to finish his sentence, but he hesitated and said nothing more. Instead, he slowly pulled his hand away.

"It was nice of you to have stopped by," he said after what Consuelo felt to be an unbearably long silence.

"It was nice of you to have invited me," she responded, immensely relieved that he hadn't actually said what he so clearly wanted to say.

Consuelo felt the evening to be peaceful and soothing as she sat on her bed writing a letter to her father. When she'd returned from Pedro's apartment, she'd quickly opened the letter her father had sent her, knowing that reading it would take her mind away from everything else. She devoured all the words that he'd written to her, enjoying the light memories they stirred and the comforting images they drew in her mind. It was only after reading the letter a second time that she set it down, placing it on the pile of all the other letters her father had sent, positioned along the wall beside her bed.

Winter was cold in Winnipeg, Consuelo then wrote to her father. Fortunately, her small apartment was well-heated and, in it, she and her daughter were warm. The snow was like nothing she'd ever seen in Chile, where it was only a far and distant coat of white on the mountains. Even though it was always so cold outside, the sun would still shine as if it were summer; it would reflect brightly off the snow and flicker back and forth on it, much like the way it would reflect off the waves that moved along the ocean.

Consuelo looked back at her daughter as she slept quietly beside her. Pilar looked so peaceful and calm, the illness in her body not giving even a hint of itself away. Perhaps the doctor was wrong, Consuelo thought to herself. Perhaps the illness that had shaken Pilar so violently a few nights ago had left her daughter's tiny body and freed it   at least, that was what she allowed herself to hope.

Consuelo noticed the snow start falling outside her window, and she stopped to watch it. It came down from the sky in a thick and light mass, with flakes bigger than any she'd ever seen before that winter, and she felt an overwhelming need to feel them against her.

She stepped out onto the balcony and allowed the flakes to fall against her skin and melt on it. She wondered if they tasted like the water in the ocean, which was so salty that it would burn your eyes to swim in it. When she opened up her mouth to catch some of the flakes, though — the flakes falling on her face and her lips before finally landing on the inside of her mouth and her tongue — they softly dissolved into fresh water, without even the slightest flavour; she hadn't expected that, and it left her unsatisfied.

20.

The water moved her peacefully and she felt protected by it. It muted almost everything else around her, letting only the deepest of sounds reach her. The therapy pool was the only place where Pilar was able to move freely without her brace; the physiotherapist had wanted her to swim around in it as much as possible to warm up her muscles and to ease her joints, but Pilar had felt so tired from the long day that instead she just allowed the water to move her as it would.

"Pilar, you're not doing it right."

Pilar was not able to make out the words completely at first, but they were repeated a few times and so she opened her eyes and saw the physiotherapist talking to her from the side of the pool.

"You need to move your legs for this to work," the therapist continued when she saw Pilar finally look up at her.

Pilar had been going to the therapist for as long as she could remember, and certainly for at least as long as she had been walking. The therapist would move her legs in different directions with her hands, instructing Pilar to push against them with all her strength — to help her walk better, or so the therapist would always tell her. Whenever the therapist would have her try to walk freely without the brace, though, Pilar still found that to be next to impossible; her left leg would simply not come under her control, no matter how much she tried.

"You have to keep trying, Pilar," the therapist would tell her. "I can see you've already given up."

Pilar wasn't certain what it was that the therapist could see, though, other than her not being able to walk correctly. She wondered why the therapist would have thought her to have given up when it was quite clear to Pilar that her body just was that way — being unable to walk well without a large metal brace clamped down around her one leg was certainly not something she had ever willed for herself.

But even with the pressure that the therapist put on her, Pilar found the therapy gym to be like a sanctuary. It kept her apart from the world outside, where she was anything other than what she should be — from the brace that she needed to walk, to the dark colour of her skin, to her mother, who spoke only the most broken fragments of English and who found it so difficult to get by in the world. At least there in the gym, Pilar was away from all that. Pilar remembered a time when she hadn't yet understood how others perceived her — but when she did come to understand that, being different was all she ever felt.

One afternoon the summer before she had started school, Pilar had watched some of the neighbourhood girls play up and down the back alley. They seemed to be having so much fun that Pilar wanted nothing more than to go down and join them. She knew that would upset her mother, though — Consuelo always insisted that it was better for her to spend her time in the apartment so that she wouldn't be physically taxed, but there were only so many things Pilar could do inside the apartment with nobody else to play with. Consuelo took her to the library a few times earlier that summer, perhaps having sensed her daughter's frustration at always having to stay inside, but it was obvious to Pilar that her mother found it difficult to be out for any significant length of time. Instead of feeling free to spend all the time she wanted exploring the library, Pilar dutifully quickly picked out a few books with some pictures that she wanted to try to copy so that her mother wouldn't have to be out for too long. Consuelo had a difficult time expressing herself in English and when it was spoken fast would often have to ask the speaker to repeat themselves just to understand, making most of her conversations slow and awkward. It was clear to Pilar that her mother preferred not to have to talk to strangers at all.

That particular afternoon it had been so hot and muggy inside the apartment that Pilar found herself unable to resist going out to join the other children after her mother had gone to take a nap.

"Why do you have that thing on your leg?" one of the girls asked as she walked towards them.

The rest of the girls suddenly stopped jumping rope and stared at Pilar.

"It's a brace," Pilar replied. "I need it to help me walk."

"It looks weird," the girl said, surprising Pilar and making her start to wonder if going out to join them had been such a good idea after all.

"Are you from Mexico?" the girl continued. "My mom says that's why your mother doesn't want to work."

The other girls around them started to giggle and Pilar had no idea what to do or say next. After another moment of glances and snickers between the girls, Pilar came to understand that they would make no room for her there.

Pilar's walk back up to her apartment felt much longer than her walk out. The mugginess of the day's heat closed in around her more and more with each step, and her left leg soon started to tighten underneath her brace. By the time she reached the apartment, Pilar found it difficult even just to stand on her leg, let alone take a step forward with the full weight of her body pushing over it.

"Pilar! Are you all right?" her mother asked, rushing up to the door just as Pilar finally made it back inside. "What happened?"

"I was playing with some of the kids outside and I tripped," Pilar explained, not even for one moment considering telling her mother the truth.

"What — ? What did your physiotherapist tell you about over-exerting your leg?"

Her mother's loud and disapproving tone overwhelmed Pilar, compounding all the disappointment she'd already felt, and she started to cry. She hadn't meant to — and certainly not in front of her mother — but needed to, regardless.

"It's all right," her mother said, her tone much softer now.

Consuelo picked Pilar up and took her to her bedroom. Pilar felt her mother struggle every now and then along the way, but she did not stop until she managed to set Pilar down on her bed. Consuelo pried off the brace from her leg and Pilar immediately started to regain a sense of comfort.

"You should try to sleep," Consuelo told her after tucking her into her bed and kissing her on the forehead. "I'll wake you for supper," she continued before leaving the room.

Whatever sense of comfort Pilar started to feel as she lay in bed, though, was completely lost when she heard her mother crying from her own bedroom next door. Pilar wasn't certain at first what the sound was because it was faint in comparison to the noises that drifted in through her open window, but when the sounds from outside died down it became clear to Pilar what it was. Pilar tried to block it out by thinking about other things, like the clock ticking on the table beside her, counting out the seconds as they passed, or focusing on the sounds that came in through her open window, of traffic and people passing by her apartment, but she found it impossible not to keep returning to the sound of her mother crying. After a while, Pilar covered her ears with her pillow, but her mother's sadness had already seeped inside her by then.

"How was your session today?" Consuelo asked when Pilar returned home from her physiotherapy session after working in the therapy pool.

"It was all right," Pilar replied; it was always all right, because that was all she ever dared tell her mother, not wanting to risk upsetting her by telling her anything more.

Consuelo used to go with her to her sessions, but stopped accompanying her from one day to the next, after the therapist had made a comment about the colour of Pilar's eyes.

"They're such an unusual shade of blue — almost translucent," Pilar overheard the therapist remark to her mother. "Are her father's eyes that colour?"

The question had seemed innocent enough to Pilar, even when she recalled it later, but it had clearly upset her mother, though she had tried not to let on.

"No," Consuelo responded to the therapist after a moment, her tone suddenly curt. "Her father did not have blue eyes."

"Your father went missing after the military overthrew the president in Chile during a coup d'etat, and nobody's heard from him since," Consuelo had told Pilar when she'd asked about her father once, after she'd first realized that everybody had not only a mother, but also a father. "The military rounded up people after they took power and did terrible things to them. Many people disappeared."

Yet even though Pilar had asked about him long before, the therapist's mention of her father that day had not only upset Consuelo, but also left her visibly disturbed long after the session had finished. Consuelo had stopped accompanying Pilar into the therapy room right after that session, opting instead to wait outside in the lounge area, and eventually stopped going all together.

"You're a big girl, now," her mother had explained to Pilar. "I'm sure the last thing you want is to have your mother hanging around with you."

"I didn't realize how long it's been since I last saw you, but look how much you've grown."

Pilar was sitting in the stairwell that afternoon, working on a drawing. She enjoyed working on her pictures in the stairwell because the light was better there, allowing her to see her lines clearly. Her mother didn't like the brightness and was always turning off the lights in the apartment and closing the drapes to shut out the light from outside, and Pilar found it difficult to draw in that environment. Pilar would often try to draw in her bedroom with the door closed, but the sensation of her mother's presence in the apartment made her uneasy — both when Pilar could hear her mother moving about, and even more so when she could not.

Pilar hadn't thought much about the man when she noticed him walking up towards her in the stairwell, assuming he was going to pass her up to the next floor. What surprised her, though, was not only that he stopped and spoke to her, but that he spoke to her in Spanish. Nobody other than her mother had ever spoken to her in Spanish before.

"You don't remember me, do you?" the man asked, having correctly interpreted her look.

Pilar thought it was the brightness of the light in the stairwell that allowed her to see the scars along the man's face so clearly when she looked up at him — if she'd met him in one of the apartment corridors or in the lobby she might not even have noticed them, because the light was more muted there. His scars were quite faded, like a memory that had been drawn into him, woven into his skin and running down along his face and neck — but they were still there to see.

"What are you drawing?" the man asked, glancing at her notebook.

"Just some stuff," Pilar responded, shrugging her shoulders.

"Well, it looks very good," he continued. "You have some real talent there."

"Thank you," Pilar replied, because she knew that was what was expected of her and not because the compliment was something she needed.

"Is that some place you know, or is it made up?"

"I guess it's a bit of both," Pilar responded, after thinking about it for a moment. She hadn't consciously thought about what it was when she was working on the drawing, but thinking about it now she realized that was what it was — she had started with the idea of the park down the street where she would sometimes stop after school when she was a bit early, but she had made the grass taller and thicker, added more shrubs and trees and turned the fountain at the centre of it into a vast pool of water in the horizon that ended only when it touched the sky.

"It reminds me of home," the man commented.

"You mean Chile?" Pilar asked. It had dawned on her that he must have been from there, just like her mother.

The man smiled and patted Pilar on the head.

"Be sure to say hello to your mother for me," he said before continuing up the stairs. "It's been a while since I've seen her, too."

"I will," Pilar said.

"I hope she's doing well," he said, turning back to look at Pilar from a few steps up.

Pilar gave him only a small smile in acknowledgement, but that seemed to be all the man needed in order to continue on his way. For some reason, Pilar sensed that he already knew exactly how her mother was doing without her having to say even one word.

"What were you doing in the stairwell?" her mother asked her at supper, after Pilar had told her about the man; she had thought that Consuelo would be interested in knowing that he'd wondered about her, but her mother's reaction was much more hostile than Pilar had anticipated.

"I was just working on some drawings," Pilar responded hesitantly, gauging from her mother's look that she was expecting an answer though Pilar wasn't certain what the right answer would be.

"What's wrong with working on your drawings here in the apartment?" her mother asked. "It's certainly a lot more comfortable than the stairwell, not to mention a lot safer."

"It's just the people from the apartment block who walk by," Pilar responded, hoping to calm her mother.

"You never know about people," Consuelo said. "It's not safe to trust anybody but your own family."

"But what about that man?" Pilar asked, surprised by her mother's sudden decisiveness.

"You should stay away from Pedro, too," Consuelo told her, not questioning for one moment who he was, her tone stopping the conversation.

Pilar sat alone in her bedroom later that evening, looking at the white walls that surrounded her — they blended into each other and into the white ceiling above them, encasing her away from everything that lay beyond. The small window facing the alley gave the only hint that there was something more in the world, and Pilar suddenly felt the need to change that. She ripped some of her drawings out of her notebook and headed out to find some tape. As she walked down the hallway, she noticed her mother in her own bedroom: Consuelo was sitting on her bed, reading a letter, the small lamp on the table beside her providing all the light she needed. Pilar hadn't noticed her mother come up with a new letter earlier that day, so Consuelo must have been reading one from before, one she was sure to have read over and over again many times by then. Pilar sometimes wondered what it was those letters contained, what stories they told or what love they offered — why it was that they drew her mother in so deeply — but Pilar never dared ask her. All Pilar knew was that they were from her grandfather, but nothing more.

"Did you want something?" Consuelo asked when she noticed Pilar looking at her.

"I'm just looking for some tape," Pilar responded.

"There's some in the kitchen drawer," her mother said, returning to her reading.

Pilar watched her mother within her own private world for another moment, wishing she could be part of what made her happy, but Consuelo offered her nothing more and so Pilar eventually continued quietly on her way.

Back in her room, Pilar taped her drawings onto the walls, wanting to be surrounded by them more than just in her mind. They made her feel as if the world was not so small and cramped, as if there was some place beyond where she was now that was waiting for her.

21.

She had found it hard to imagine the way he'd described it: "It's when a stone that's just forming gradually takes the place of something that had once lived and then died, turning it into part of the stone with it."

He had just started to pull it out of his pocket when the teacher looked back at them and interrupted them.

"Is there something you'd like to share with the rest of the class, Simon?" the teacher asked.

"No, Miss St. Pierre," Simon responded, quickly tucking the stone back into his pocket before Pilar could get a good look at it.

Pilar tried to catch Simon's attention again a few times later during class, long after the teacher had returned to her desk, but Simon didn't turn back to Pilar again. Pilar wanted so much to have a look at the stone for herself, but worried that Simon might have changed his mind about letting her see it the way he ignored her for the rest of the class.

It was only at the end of the day that Simon finally spoke to her again. He left the classroom right after the buzzer rang without stopping to wait for Pilar like he normally would, but when Pilar got outside, he was there waiting for her. Simon held out the stone for her as soon as he saw her, knowing without her needing to say one word that it was what she wanted.

"Look at the two of them: the geek and the spaz!" one of the children said to some of the others as they walked out the school doors, speaking loud enough for Pilar and Simon to overhear.

Pilar wasn't certain which one in the group had said it, but it didn't matter because it could have been any one of them on any given day. It didn't bother Pilar so much for herself, but it did make her feel sorry for Simon — she was used to the other kids teasing her because of how she walked with her brace and how she looked, but Simon was clearly stunned by the comment, as if it had been the last thing he'd expected to hear.

After the kids had left, Simon gave Pilar a weak half-smile and then quietly walked off by himself. Pilar wanted to say something that would make him feel better, but thought it would probably be best to let him be, just like she'd learned to do for her mother in those moments when sadness would clearly overwhelm her.

When Pilar had first met Simon, there wasn't any one thing in particular that caught her attention about him, except that he was quiet and distant. The teacher had explained to the rest of the third-grade class that he'd transferred in from another school and that they should all help him feel welcome, but it was clear even on that first day that he preferred to stay to himself as much as possible. For that reason Pilar hadn't expected him to walk right up to her one day after school while she was drawing some pictures as she waited for the bus.

"How can you draw like that?" he asked when she looked up at him. "Did somebody teach you?"

"No, nobody taught me," Pilar replied. "I don't know why I can draw like this," she added after a moment, having gauged by Simon's expression that he was left unsatisfied by her first response.

Pilar had understood for some time that it was unusual to be able to draw the way she did, with her hand following through so accurately on the images and thoughts in her mind. It was something that had just happened on its own, though, without any conscious effort on her part, and so she was not able to explain it to others. Simon had walked off after that with a disappointed smile, and she was left wondering if he'd thought her response to have been insincere.

Simon was moody and inconsistent at the best of times, sometimes taking the time to talk to her and expressing interest in what she was drawing or what they were working on in school, and other times completely ignoring her as if he didn't know her. In many ways, he reminded Pilar of her mother and so she didn't think his sudden distance meant anything in particular, other than that he was sad.

A few weeks earlier, Pilar had caught a glimpse of Simon with his mother in the school corridor as she walked with her own mother to their parent-teacher meeting.

"Just wait until your father finds out you've been talking in class instead of listening to the teacher," Pilar overheard a woman say as she and her mother approached the classroom. "You're going to be in real trouble then."

Pilar turned towards the voice and noticed Simon farther off down the hall walking alongside a woman Pilar presumed to be his mother. Just before they vanished around the corner,

Simon met Pilar's look, allowing her to see his sadness in that brief moment.

"It's good to see that you've made a new friend, Pilar," Miss St. Pierre said to Pilar just as her meeting with her mother was finishing up. "But you have to remember to hold your personal conversations outside of class."

"Yes, Miss St. Pierre," Pilar responded quietly, surprised by how calmly and inconspicuously the teacher had mentioned it.

Pilar had worried during the whole meeting that the teacher would bring up her talking to Simon in class and request that she be punished for it. Simon was always quiet in class, speaking only to her, and so if his mother was upset about his talking in class, Pilar thought it had to be because the teacher had complained and she was certain the same fate awaited her. Instead, though, the teacher had brought it up almost as an after-thought and Pilar was left wondering if that small comment was what could have made Simon's mother so upset.

"You didn't mention having a friend," Consuelo remarked as they stepped out into the hallway after the meeting had finished.

"He's just a boy in class," Pilar said, shrugging. "We just talk sometimes."

"That's nice," her mother replied, surprising Pilar with how relieved she sounded.

When Pilar saw Simon the following day, she thought it best not to mention anything about the evening before. He could not have known how much of his mother's words she'd actually heard, and Pilar thought that if she didn't let on, perhaps he would think that she hadn't heard any of it at all. He was silent and moody again that day. Pilar knew there was nothing she could say that would change anything for him, and so she offered him her own silence instead.

"It's a fossil," he told her.

"What's that?"

"Well, the stone formed around the butterfly over a long period of time," Pedro explained.

"But how did it become a stone?" Pilar asked after thinking about it for a moment.

"That I know with one-hundred-percent certainty, because I happen to be studying that very thing in my class," he said.

Pedro took a seat beside her on the bench and pulled a large text book out of his bag, opening it up to some illustrations.

"These are the layers of the earth," he said, pointing to one of the pictures. "There are always new layers building up on top of the old ones, and the weight of all the new layers can turn the old layers into stone. Anything caught in the layers during this process can turn into a fossil."

"But why was the butterfly in the earth?" Pilar asked, still not understanding.

"Because it had lived its life, and then died, Pilar," Pedro said after hesitating for a moment. "But don't worry, its soul flew off long ago to heaven."

"Oh," she replied, looking down again at the stone in her hand. "Aren't you too old to be going to school?" Pilar asked after a moment, as she watched Pedro put his book back into his bag.

"Probably," he replied. "But it's what I have to do."

"Why?"

"Because I want to get a better job and what I studied in Chile doesn't count here."

"Because you studied it in Spanish?" Pilar asked.

"Kind of," Pedro replied. "You shouldn't stay out here alone — it's not safe to be here after dark," he continued as he got up.

"I want to finish up this drawing before supper," Pilar explained. "I'm just going to stay here for a little while longer."

"All right," Pedro said. "But just a few minutes," he insisted before heading off to the apartment block himself.

When Pilar went home a short while later, she carefully tucked the stone away in her night table drawer, not wanting to risk losing it.

"Pilar," her mother called out from the kitchen. "Your supper's getting cold."

"I'm just in my room," Pilar answered as she heard her mother approach.

"Do you have homework you need to finish up?" her mother asked, walking up to her doorway just as Pilar shut her drawer.

"No, I finished it all in class."

"Were you working on some drawings?" Consuelo asked.

Pilar nodded in response but offered nothing more, worried about upsetting her mother if she told her she'd spoken to Pedro.

"What did you work on?"

"Just some sketches," Pilar replied, handing her mother some of the drawings, hoping they would quell her curiosity.

"A butterfly — ?" her mother asked after a moment, flipping through the pages.

"Yes," Pilar responded. "I found a butterfly fossil and drew it with some different ideas, mainly with different textures."

"They're very nice," her mother said after looking at the drawings for a moment longer and then quietly handing them back to her daughter.

Consuelo left Pilar's room without saying anything more, neither there, nor later as they ate. After supper, Consuelo quickly disappeared into her bedroom. Though Pilar didn't find anything specifically unusual about her mother's behaviour, she sensed that something had upset her mother, but she didn't know what.

That night, her mother was restless. Through the wall between their rooms, Pilar could hear Consuelo moving around, seeming to be searching for something. Then, suddenly, all the sounds stopped. Pilar couldn't remember falling asleep, but then she was suddenly woken in the middle of the night by her mother screaming.

"Mom?" Pilar called out, putting on her brace and heading over to her mother's room as fast as she could.

Consuelo had already turned on the light by the time Pilar reached her door; she was sitting up in her bed, visibly startled.

"What happened?" Pilar asked.

"I must have had a nightmare," Consuelo replied. "But I really can't remember."

"Are you all right?"

Even though Consuelo smiled and nodded in response, Pilar could tell that her mother was quite shaken.

"Let me help you back to bed," her mother said, turning the topic of conversation away from herself. "You need to get a full night's rest for school tomorrow."

When her mother stood up, Pilar noticed something on the night table beside her bed — a small wooden case with a glass cover. It caught her attention because she did not remember ever seeing it in her mother's room before. She tried to get a better look at it, but was unable to do so as her mother led her out the door.

The next morning when her mother was distracted making breakfast, Pilar thought she had the perfect opportunity to get a better look at the small wooden box. When she peered into her mother's bedroom from the hallway, though, the case was gone from the night table and was nowhere in sight.

"Your tea's ready," her mother called out to her.

Pilar turned back to the kitchen and saw her mother sitting at the table, waiting for her. If Consuelo had noticed what Pilar had been trying to see, however, she did not give any sign of that away.

Pilar stared at the stone again days later as she lay in bed before going to sleep. She had taken the stone with her to school all week wanting to return it to Simon, but he did not show up for even one day and so she finally decided to keep it tucked safely in her drawer until she was certain he would be there. Pilar carefully traced the image on the stone with her finger, feeling the texture of it: the sharp edges followed by the smoothness of the stone. She found it hard to resist looking at it, finding the idea so curious — how it could actually not be there, and yet its shape and form still remain so clear. She wondered how it could have left itself, how its body could exist without any real remnant of what it had been. She wondered if the butterfly could really exist in heaven without its body — without its senses to guide it and define it for itself. Without its butterfly body, she wondered if it could still feel the wind when it flew; without its butterfly wings, was it able to feel the warmth of the sun?

At least the butterfly had been free to move and feel while it had been alive, Pilar thought. She wondered if the same had ever been true of her mother — if Consuelo had ever allowed herself to move and feel and experience life, before she turned into a remnant of herself. Pilar wondered if her mother had ever even been capable of those things.

22.

The door creaked loudly when she returned home from supper that evening, though she had not wanted anything to disturb her mother from her rest.

"Did you have supper?" Pilar heard Consuelo's voice from down the hall.

The sensation of her mother's overwhelming sorrow flooded into the hallway as Consuelo walked out of her room to greet her daughter, and quickly moved in to envelop Pilar within it.

"Yes, I had supper," Pilar managed to reply after a moment.

"There's food in the fridge if you're still hungry."

"I'm not hungry."

Consuelo continued looking at Pilar for a moment and then retreated back down the hall and into her room; she moved slowly and quietly, yet there was nothing light about her.

Pilar had sensed that morning that there was something wrong by the way her mother had spoken on the phone, suddenly hesitating shortly after she'd started to speak.

"Hurry up, Pilar," Consuelo said after a moment, covering the phone receiver with her hand, sounding agitated. "You're going to miss your bus."

Pilar looked back at the clock wondering how she could have misjudged the time so much that morning, but then saw that she wasn't late at all. Her mother's continued stare, though, made her get up from the table, get her books and head out for the day. Pilar felt her mother's eyes following her the whole time she was getting ready to leave, but she didn't dare meet them again.

Because of her mother's odd behaviour that morning, Pilar wasn't surprised to find Pedro in the living room when she returned home from school that afternoon. He was sitting on the sofa reading a newspaper, but seemed to be waiting specifically for her because he started packing everything back into his bag as soon as she walked in.

"Your mother asked me to take you out for supper," he told her.

Pilar looked over at her mother's bedroom door — the door was closed and all she could see were the dark shadows in the hallway in front of it.

"Is she all right?" Pilar asked, looking back at Pedro.

"She's just a bit tired and needs some rest."

"Oh," Pilar said, glancing back at her mother's closed door again, Pedro's words having done nothing to reassure her.

"What did you learn in school today?" he asked, after ordering hamburgers for the two of them at the restaurant down the street and they'd sat in silence for a moment.

Pilar just shrugged her shoulders in response, finding it odd that Pedro was behaving as though there was nothing unusual in their supper out.

"Okay," Pedro continued after a moment, pulling out a book from his bag. "Then I can show you what I learned."

When Pedro started flipping through the pages of his book, Pilar noticed it was the same one he'd shown her weeks earlier, when he'd explained the fossil to her. This time, though, he stopped on a page with all sorts of different coloured shapes.

"Do you know what this is?" he asked.

Pilar gave Pedro a blank look in response, not understanding what all the different colours meant.

"It's a map of the world," Pedro told her. "These coloured shapes are the different continents where all the people in the world live."

Pilar tried to make out from the picture what it was that he was explaining to her, but she simply was not able to see it; she couldn't understand what separated one colour from another, and why there were so many different isolated colours in small shapes and yet so much blue.

"It's the ocean," Pedro told her after she'd asked him about it.

"What's that?"

Pedro leaned back in his seat then and looked at her as though he were at a complete loss for words.

"Why do you want to go down there?" Simon asked Pilar, following her down the street that day at lunch.

"I don't know," she replied; the truth was she wasn't sure she could fully explain it to him. "I just want to go down and look at the water."

"By the time you get down there, it'll just be time to come back again."

Pilar just shrugged her shoulders in response, unswayed by his words. Simon's curiosity must have gotten the better of him, though, because he kept following her.

Simon had returned to classes a few weeks earlier, two weeks to the day after he'd given her the stone, but he hadn't talked much to Pilar since then.

"I was sick," he told her when he first returned, after she'd asked him why he'd been away for so long.

"It must have been very bad," Pilar commented.

"It was," he replied, something in his tone telling Pilar that he wasn't interested in discussing it anymore, and so she left it at that.

"I can bring your stone back tomorrow," she told him after a moment. "I didn't know you were going to be here today."

"That's okay; I didn't expect you to give it back."

"Do you know what it is?" she asked him, suddenly curious to know that.

"What do you mean?"

"Did you know it's actually a real butterfly that was caught in the stone?" she continued.

"The fossil — ?" Simon asked, making it perfectly clear with that he did know what it was. "But it's not that it got caught in the stone, Pilar — the butterfly became the stone."

Pilar looked at him, confused. "The butterfly went to heaven after it died," she told him.

"If you believe in heaven," Simon responded.

"And if you don't — ?" Pilar asked.

"If you don't, you know that the very components that made up the butterfly moved on to become different parts of different things — some pieces becoming part of the stone and other pieces turning into the things around it, like the wind and the air, and maybe even the rain after it fell down on it."

That night, Pilar replayed Simon's words over and over again in her mind, the idea making so much more sense to her than Pedro's explanation. She had seen it, the way dead birds on sidewalks or in the alleys would slowly disintegrate over time, becoming scrawny and deflated versions of themselves with only their skeletons and some feathers remaining, but she had never really thought about what had happened to the rest of them, to the pieces that were no longer there. Simon's words had made her think of her grandfather and what he had become through his dying. She wondered what the pieces of him had already turned into and what the rest would, in time. Would he become a stone like the butterfly, or something else entirely? Perhaps the rain had already carried some of his elements down the rivers and the streams, to eventually go everywhere and become part of everything, in time.

It did not take Pilar long after Pedro had first taken her out for supper to figure out why her mother had grown so suddenly despondent. She didn't realize it right away when her mother stopped waking in the mornings to make her breakfast — her mother sometimes felt ill and so that wasn't entirely unusual. It was when her mother stopped going down to check for the mail each day that Pilar started to understand.

A few days after her mother had received that early morning phone call, Pilar noticed mail still in the box when she returned home from school — there were a few bills and also a letter she was certain was from her grandfather. She took that letter right up to her mother, certain that she could want to read it right away, but instead of taking it and quickly absorbing every word it contained, Consuelo asked Pilar to set it on the stack of all the other letters from her father, leaving it unopened. Her mother just stared at it from where she sat on her bed, giving Pilar the sense that she was afraid of it.

"Do you have any homework?" Consuelo asked Pilar after a moment; she did not turn to look at Pilar, though, and with her words made it clear that she wanted to be left alone.

After that one letter, there were no more. When more days had passed than had ever separated her grandfather's letters from one another before, it occurred to Pilar then that there would be no more. That was why Pilar wanted to go to the river that day at lunch, though she found herself incapable of explaining it to Simon: she wanted to know if she could find some small fragments of her grandfather within the flowing water. If she took some of the water back home, perhaps her mother would somehow feel her father's presence within the world and not be so sad any more.

Pilar watched Simon dip the jar into the river and fill it up with water. Pilar had tried to get closer to the shore herself, but it was too uneven, filled with rocks and shrubs and deep cracks, and she wasn't able to manoeuvre her braced leg around them.

"Is this enough?" Simon asked from the shoreline, holding up the almost-full jar for Pilar to see.

Pilar nodded, certain it would be.

"You know it won't last long in there," Simon told her after tightening the lid and handing her the jar. "There's a lot of stuff in the water that's so small you might not see it, but it's full of life."

"I know," Pilar replied, carefully taking the jar and putting it into her backpack.

Alone in her bedroom that night, she opened the jar. She then pulled out the new paint set which Pedro had bought her just the evening before when they'd gone to the mall for supper. The craft store had caught her attention on the way in, with the vibrant colours of the pencils and the papers in the display window, but it was on the opposite side from where they walked in and she wasn't able to get a close look. On the way out, she asked Pedro if they could walk over, having been able to think of nothing else as she'd eaten. More than the pencils and the papers, though, it was the paints that had mesmerized her — the small circles of colour stood out so brightly and the blue of it matched perfectly the colour of the ocean in the map Pedro had shown her.

"Have you used water colours before?" Pedro asked as he watched her stare at the paints.

"In school," Pilar replied.

"And how about at home?" he asked.

"I use the pencil set Mom bought me for school."

"Maybe you can try the paints at home, too," he said, taking her hand and leading her into the store.

Now in her room, Pilar dipped her paintbrush into the river water and then brushed it over the blue circle, creating a sudden pool of thick blue liquid on top of it. She smoothed the paint out onto the white paper and then watched as its fibres soaked up the colour of it. When she dipped the brush back into the water a second time, it drew out the blue left on the brush and absorbed it; and when she stirred the brush within it, the water turned completely blue. Pilar stared at the water for a moment, struck by how quickly it had allowed the paint to seep through and change it. Eventually, she continued painting again until there was no blue paint left except for a few stains in the white plastic holder that had contained it. She then put the lid back on the jar and returned it to her backpack to take back down to the river — even though she had changed the colour of what remained of it, she thought it would be best to return it to where it had come from, so that it could continue along as it was meant to travel.

When the sheets of painted paper had dried, Pilar taped them up on the wall between her and her mother's bedrooms. That wall had let many sounds and feelings pass through it, to the point of disturbing Pilar's sleep; if all those things could move from her mother's bedroom into hers, then surely things could move the other way also. Pilar hoped that somehow her mother would be able to feel the fragments of water seep through to her and sense her father's presence that way — if not while she was awake, maybe in her sleep, in the moments when she was able to dream, and in that way be comforted.

23.

Her mother's room was dark, even with the bedside light on; the light illuminated only a small part of the room but did not go beyond, as if it didn't dare.

"Mom?" Pilar called from the doorway.

When Consuelo turned, it became clear to Pilar that even though her mother hadn't responded to her knocking a few moments earlier, it wasn't because she had been asleep.

"Did you want something to eat?" Pilar asked. "I was just going to make some supper."

Her mother offered her only a small smile.

"You have to eat something," Pilar continued after a moment, frustrated with her mother's lack of response.

"Really, I'm not hungry," Consuelo replied in a quiet voice.

"Have you eaten anything at all today?"

Consuelo looked down for a moment, as if needing to think about the answer. "You can bring me some tea if you'd like," she finally allowed.

In the few years that had passed since her grandfather had died, her mother had grown even more reclusive than before, but she had grown noticeably weaker and more fatigued in the past few weeks and this had started to worry Pilar. Consuelo no longer made any effort to get up to greet Pilar when she returned home from school and she didn't seem to care to eat at all; when she did eat, it seemed to be more as an effort to assuage Pilar, but because Pilar sensed that, it did nothing to alleviate her concern.

"How long has she been like that?" Pedro asked after Pilar finally decided to tell him, having felt the need to tell somebody.

"A few weeks."

"Does she get up at all?"

"Sometimes, but not much."

"Has she gone to see the doctor?"

"No, I don't think so," Pilar replied, the idea not having occurred to her before.

Pilar wasn't certain what Pedro said to her mother when they returned home that evening — Pedro having insisted on going into Consuelo's bedroom to speak with her, although Pilar hadn't thought that would be a good idea — but when Pilar returned home from school the next day, her mother was out of bed and gone from the apartment. She must have started to feel better, Pilar thought. Perhaps her mother had simply had a flu and had only needed some time to sleep it off. Pilar started to feel silly for having been so concerned and for having said anything to Pedro, certain that he had better things to do than to indulge her worries. Regardless, Pilar was relieved that her mother had finally gotten up, for some air and movement.

The open door to her mother's room was the first thing that caught Pilar's attention when she returned home that afternoon. She noticed the perfectly made bed and the daylight streaming in through the window with its open drapes, lighting up more of the room than Pilar had ever seen before. She couldn't help but stare at everything, not having expected how easily her mother's room had accepted light within it.

Pilar had often wondered what it was that her mother kept tucked away in the darkened corners of her room, and her curiosity pulled her in further. She wondered if her mother had anything that gave her comfort, or if that was even something that Consuelo was capable of feeling. Pilar glanced back to the open bedroom doorway behind her before stepping in further, needing to be absolutely sure that she was alone, knowing that she shouldn't be doing the very thing she was going to do.

Her mother's night table drawer slid out smoothly and easily, to Pilar's surprise. The drawer was filled with papers and documents, but it was the small red booklet that stood out the most: the old Chilean passport that her mother had used for her travel to Canada. As Pilar flipped through its pages, carefully reading each one and absorbing all the information it contained, she realized that Consuelo had been just a few years older than Pilar herself was now when she'd come to Canada. Her mother had always seemed so old to Pilar, but in actuality she was quite young. When Pilar reached the page in the passport with the photograph of her mother fifteen years earlier, she couldn't take her eyes off it, struck by how stunningly beautiful her mother had once been. Though Pilar recognized her mother in the photograph, the beauty wasn't something she'd expected because there was no trace of it left, not for as long as Pilar could remember.

Deeper inside the drawer, Pilar found a small jewellery case with a tiny, delicate necklace inside. It picked up the light of the room and reflected it back brightly when Pilar picked it up for a better look, and Pilar found it curious that her mother would keep such a beautiful necklace so close to her and yet never wear it.

When Pilar looked up from the drawer, she noticed her mother's closet door was slightly ajar and saw boxes inside it, lined up along the floor. The first box was full of the letters that her grandfather had sent to her mother, which Consuelo had packed away shortly after his death. Pilar remembered that after years of lining her mother's wall, they were suddenly all gone one day, but she hadn't dared ask her mother what had happened to them even though she was curious. The second box was also full of letters, as was the third, but on top of the letters in the third box there was a small wooden case with a glass cover and three butterflies with their wings pinned open inside of it. Pilar knew instantly that it was the same case she'd seen the night her mother had woken up screaming years earlier — Pilar hadn't been able to get a close look at it then, but she remembered its wooden edges and glass cover.

Pilar had just started to pull it out to get a better look at it when she heard knocking on the front door, followed by the sound of the door being unlocked. Pilar froze, scared that her mother would find her rummaging through her things.

"Pilar, are you here?" she heard Pedro call out, the sound of his voice coming as an instant relief to her.

"I'll be out in a second," she replied, quickly putting all her mother's things back to their proper places before heading out to the hall to meet him.

"I'm going to take you to the hospital," he told her as she walked up to him. "They've admitted your mother for some tests."

"The hospital — ?"

"They just want to find out why she's been feeling so tired," Pedro replied, his words intending to put Pilar at ease, but not succeeding.

Her mother's eyes were closed when they entered her room and this made Pilar think that she was asleep, but then Consuelo opened them suddenly and easily, and it became apparent to Pilar that she hadn't been sleeping at all. Perhaps her mother had been thinking about something and had closed her eyes to help her concentrate, Pilar thought.

The hospital room was small, with barely enough space for all the things contained within it. Beside her mother's bed there were two small chairs, and behind those was a curtain separating her mother from the woman in the bed beside her. There was nothing welcoming about the space or its artificial lights — under them, Consuelo looked even more tired than before, her skin a greenish hue.

"I've been waiting for you to come," Consuelo said to Pilar, smiling.

"Why are you here?" Pilar asked, looking at the monitor wired to her mother and the tube feeding into her hand.

Consuelo glanced up at Pedro, as if looking for the answer from him. Only after that did she respond to Pilar's question, the expression on Pedro's face seeming to have spoken something to her, silently. "They're trying to make me better."

Pilar looked at her mother and studied her expression, then looked up at Pedro, following her mother's own look. She wondered what they were both obviously hiding from her.

"Did you finish your homework?" her mother asked.

Pilar nodded; in truth she hadn't even begun, but the idea of it now was utterly unimportant to her.

"Why don't you sit by me here?" Consuelo suggested, motioning to the chair beside her, and so Pilar did, Pedro moving quickly to help her with the chair and then quietly leaving the room.

Consuelo caressed her daughter's face and the feel of Consuelo's hand against her skin moved Pilar, with the softness and the care that it carried. Until that moment Pilar had believed that in the hospital her mother would be cured of whatever it was that had made her sick. The way her mother touched her face now, though, was unfamiliar and it left Pilar no longer certain of anything. It was the heaviness behind her mother's touch that made her sense that something was very wrong — it lingered, as if her mother wanted to hold onto that one moment for as long as possible, needing for it to be suspended from time.

The intense longing of that moment reminded Pilar of the last time she'd seen Simon. He had visited her a few times at the apartment the summer before they were to change schools for high school, asking her about the pictures she was working on and even accompanying her out to the park while she drew. He often came by with cuts and bruises on his face and his arms, sometimes trying to cover them up and other times not bothering — regardless, though, Pilar knew enough never to ask him about them. Simon never talked about his bruises or how they came to be, but Pilar felt that it was not because he was trying to deny their existence, but rather because their existence was something beyond his control, just like the brace on her leg was for her.

"Do you think you'll ever get to see the ocean?" he asked her one afternoon in the park.

"I don't know," Pilar responded, never having even considered the possibility. "It's pretty far away."

"Then why do you draw it so much?"

Pilar shrugged in response, not certain she understood the reason herself.

"Do you know what you would do if you ever did see it?" Simon continued after a while, watching Pilar work on her drawings some more. "If it was right in front of you, so close that you could touch it?"

"I guess I've never really thought about it," Pilar answered.

"I know what I would do," he said. "I would walk in and float away."

"Where would you go?"

Simon was silent for a long moment — if Pilar didn't know Simon she might have wondered if he'd heard her question, but she knew he had and so she just allowed the silence to exist between them as she waited for his response.

"Wherever the water would want to take me, I suppose — so long as it's far away from here," he finally responded, not looking at Pilar or at anything in particular.

Pilar looked at Simon after he'd spoken, uncertain if there was anything she could possibly offer him. Suddenly, without fully understanding why, she leaned over and kissed him lightly and softly on the cheek — it wasn't something that she'd thought about before doing, but rather was something she'd felt the need to do in that moment.

After her kiss, Simon turned and looked at Pilar for the longest while without saying or doing anything and without even the smallest change of expression. Pilar wondered if he understood what love was or if he was even capable of receiving it. After a long moment of nothing but silence between them, Pilar understood that their conversation had ended and so she decided to continue with her drawing. Simon stayed with her there until after the sun had fallen, when she knew that her mother would be expecting her.

"I should get back home before my mother starts to worry," she told him as she started to get up.

Simon moved quickly to help her, as courteous as always, but then stayed behind when she started to walk towards the apartment block.

"I'll keep an eye out for you to make sure that you're safe," he said when she looked back at him curiously. "I'm going to stay out here for a while longer."

It was weeks before she saw him again, when school had started that fall. Though she immediately recognized him when he walked into class, something about him seemed to have changed profoundly. It was nothing about his physical appearance, but rather something at the very core of his being that emanated out from him — all the softness was gone from his expression and the way he carried himself, and he was left only with hard edges. Soon, he started to get sent to the vice principal's office regularly for talking back to the teachers and for fighting with other kids in the hall, and some days he would spend more time in detention than in class. Then one day he stopped showing up to school altogether.

Pilar hadn't seen Simon for a few years when she bumped into him again as she was leaving school just a few weeks before her mother was hospitalized. He was the furthest thing from her mind when he walked into the main foyer at the same moment she was about to leave, and they both stopped and looked at each other. For some reason, just his presence made Pilar very self-conscious.

"I didn't expect to see you here," Simon said. "I thought maybe you'd have skipped a few grades by now and would already have been long gone to university."

"I wish," Pilar replied, immensely relieved that he had spoken first. "I haven't seen you around in a while," she added, that moment between them seeming uncomplicated and honest to her, and so she'd dared more.

Simon smiled, and hesitated — the gesture reminding Pilar so much of the little boy she remembered him being once.

"I had some stuff," he finally replied, seeming to know that Pilar would understand all that he'd left unspoken.

"You're back now?" Pilar asked, curious.

"I can't get a job if I don't finish high school," he told her. "I thought maybe I would take some shop classes."

"Shop — ? I thought you always wanted to go to university?"

"Yeah, that I did," he said. "But that was before I figured out that there are some things in life that just aren't ever going to happen, no matter how much you want them."

Pilar looked down, finding the sadness that accompanied his words too much to bear. She disappointed herself with her response, though — she wished she could have challenged him, but instead found herself unable to offer him anything at all.

"I guess I should be going," she heard Simon say. "I don't think it's a good idea to keep the vice principal waiting."

"No, I guess not," Pilar responded, only then looking back up at him but still not daring to look directly at his eyes.

Pilar watched Simon leave. He walked down the hallway and grew more distant with every step, until he was almost indistinguishable from all his surroundings. It had been so simple the way it had happened, she thought to herself — the way that he had once been so much a part of her life and yet had vanished so easily from it. Pilar finally pushed the door open and headed out to wait for her bus, having found herself looking only at the memory of Simon down the hallway and nothing that was actually real any more.

Now, in the hospital with her mother beside her, Pilar could not shake the feeling of how similar those two moments were, both leaving her with the sense of impending and inevitable loss. Even though her mother had tried to reassure her that everything would be fine, that feeling remained with Pilar as day turned into evening, staying with her long after she'd gone home for the night, disturbing her right up to the last moment she remembered before falling asleep.

24.

From where she sat in the hallway, all Pilar could see was the door that separated her from her mother. Pedro had tried his best to take her mind off what had just happened with his books and stories, but the only thing Pilar could think of was how hurt she felt that her mother had asked her to leave.

It was almost two weeks since her mother had been hospitalized and Pilar had grown into a new routine with Pedro taking her every morning to see her mother, himself having taken time off work to help the two of them. That morning, though, instead of going to the hospital they headed out to the airport. Pedro had told her very little of what they were going to do there, only that they had to pick somebody up but without explaining who it was or why.

Pilar was surprised by the man who walked up to her and Pedro as they watched the passengers come down the escalators at the arrivals gate — he was a large man with long dark curly hair and he stopped right in front of Pilar without the slightest hesitation. The man stared right into her eyes as if they told him something, and not knowing what they gave away to him made Pilar feel very uneasy.

"You must be Pilar," the man said, seeming to have sensed her nervousness and wanting to explain himself — but that he spoke to her in Spanish only served to surprise her more; Spanish was a private language she shared with her mother and with Pedro, and that this man spoke it to her now made her feel unsettled.

"Pilar can be shy sometimes," Pedro explained to the man after a moment of silence.

"You must be Pedro," the man said, offering his hand for Pedro to shake. "I'm Angel Torres."

It was only then that the whispers Pilar had overheard between her mother and Pedro in the hospital a week earlier suddenly made sense — Pedro had taken some papers from his jacket pocket and was handing them to Consuelo when Pilar managed to overhear some of their whispers. Pilar was able to make out her mother's plea to Pedro: *Promise me you'll call the angel.* At least, that was what Pilar had thought she'd heard her mother say, even though the words hadn't really made any sense to her.

"I'm so very honoured to meet you," Pedro said as he shook Angel's hand. "My brother sends me magazines from Chile so that I can keep up to date with everything that's happening back there," he added.

Pilar did not understand what exactly Pedro had meant with his words or why he would have been so honoured to meet that man, but Angel nodded in understanding, himself seeming to have needed no further clarification.

Angel briefly glanced down at Pilar, then looked back up at Pedro again. "And Consuelo?" he asked.

"I'll take you to see her right now," Pedro said.

"Did you come from Chile?" Pilar asked Angel as Pedro started to help him with his luggage, the thought having occurred to her only when Angel was unable to respond to a woman who asked him in English for the time — instead, Angel looked at Pedro curiously and Pedro responded to the woman.

"Yes, I did," Angel answered Pilar.

"To see my mother?"

"Yes."

"You know her, then?" Pilar asked, having suspected that already.

"She's my cousin.

"Oh," Pilar replied, not having expected that response from him. "Is that your real name?" she continued again after a brief moment, his name having seemed odd to her from the moment he'd first spoken it.

"Angel?" he asked curiously, to which Pilar nodded.

Angel looked at Pedro then, seeming confused by Pilar's question.

"Angel's a common name in Spanish for men," Pedro told Pilar, obviously having understood the reason for her question himself.

"Oh."

After that, there was only silence between them all. From the back seat of Pedro's car, Pilar studied as much as she could of Angel's face, to see if she could find any resemblance to her mother, but she could not — Consuelo had light, fine features and straight hair, and Angel seemed to be the exact opposite of her in almost every way. Instead of asking anything more, though, Pilar decided to sit back in her seat and watch the world outside as they quickly drove through it, understanding that what was to pass, would come to pass.

When they arrived at the hospital, Consuelo just stared at Angel as he stood in the doorway, speechless, almost in disbelief.

"Why didn't you tell me that he was coming today?" Consuelo asked Pedro as she quickly sat up in bed and tried to straighten her hair.

"You already had enough things to worry about," Pedro replied.

"Look at me, I must be such a mess — " Consuelo said, seeming to be speaking to Angel only even though she wasn't specifically looking at him.

Pilar found her mother's reaction curious, because she'd never known her to concern herself with her appearance before. Angel just kept looking at Consuelo from the doorway without saying a word. When Consuelo did finally look back up at him and met his stare, she started to cry.

"Consuelo, don't — " Angel said, only then stepping further into the room, quickly moving to her mother's side.

"Look at me," Consuelo blurted out as she cried.

"Why don't we wait outside?" Pilar heard Pedro suggest, not realizing that he'd meant his words for her. "Pilar — ?" he continued after a moment, and it was only then that she understood what he wanted.

Pilar turned back and looked at Pedro, stunned that he'd felt it appropriate to even make such a suggestion.

"Maybe that would be best," Pilar heard Consuelo say.

Pilar looked back at her mother, deeply hurt that she wanted her to leave. Her mother gave her a small smile that quietly urged her to cede, but offered nothing more by way of an explanation. Pilar looked over at Angel again, not understanding why her mother would suddenly prefer the presence of a person she hadn't seen in fifteen years or maybe even longer, over her own daughter.

"Come on, Pilar," Pedro called to her again, daring to interrupt the awkward silence. "I have a new map I've been meaning to show you. It shows all the oceans of the world so much better than the old one."

"Why did he come?" Pilar asked Pedro as they sat outside in the hallway now, turning back to him after staring at the closed door to her mother's room for a while. "Why did she want him to come?"

Pedro hesitated for a moment, seeming uncertain how to answer her question. He, too, glanced back at the closed door to Consuelo's room before turning back to look at Pilar.

"Your mother has cancer," Pedro finally allowed. "They don't know how long she's had it, but it's spread all over her body now."

"Does that mean she's sick?" Pilar asked.

"Yes. Very sick."

Pilar looked down at her feet as they swayed back and forth in front of her, not needing to ask Pedro anything more.

That evening, after Pedro had driven them home, Pilar was surprised to find that Angel would not only be staying in the apartment with her, but that he would be sleeping in her mother's bedroom, those arrangements having been made without anybody having asked her if she'd be comfortable with that.

"Did you draw those?" Angel asked her, following her to her bedroom doorway and stopping when he noticed all the drawings taped up on her walls.

"Yes."

"They're very good," he said, stepping further into her room to get a better look. "Is that some place you know?" he asked after a moment.

Pilar shrugged her shoulders evasively, not especially interested in discussing her drawings with him.

"It looks a lot like Chile," Angel continued after a moment, unaffected by her lack of response.

"That's what Pedro said," Pilar told him, needing to let him know that he'd offered her nothing new.

Angel then looked at the sheets of blue along her other wall for a moment, but said nothing more about the pictures before leaving her room.

"Good night," he said as he walked out the door, without giving Pilar the opportunity to respond before he was gone from her sight, seeming to know already that she would not.

Pilar didn't sleep well that night, unable to take her focus off the strange sounds that came from within the apartment, and especially those from her mother's bedroom. When she went to the bathroom earlier before going to bed, she had noticed light streaming out from under her mother's closed bedroom door and she was struck by how unusual that was. Later, as she tried to get to sleep, she could hear movements from the other side of the wall. She was able to make out some of the sounds, like the drawer opening and closing, but she could only guess about others, like the muted shuffling noises and sudden loud squeals, perhaps of tape or of something being ripped open. The sounds made her feel invaded within her surroundings, and yet she felt completely helpless to do anything about it.

"He's staying in your bedroom," Pilar told her mother the next morning, after Pedro and Angel had finally allowed them some time alone together.

"I know," Consuelo replied, not at all surprised or concerned, and certainly not responding in the way Pilar had hoped she would. "I told him to stay there — my bed is perfectly good and it's not being used."

Pilar looked down at the ground then, left at a loss for words and not wanting her mother to see her disappointment. When she felt her mother's hand softly caressing her face, though, she knew that her mother had felt it anyway.

"I'm very sick," Consuelo told her after a moment, in a soft and apologetic tone.

"Pedro said you have cancer," Pilar allowed, not daring to look up at her mother as she spoke — she did not know how she would react if she met her mother's look and she did not want to cry in front of her.

"You're not going to have to worry about anything," her mother continued. "You're going to be very well looked after."

At first Pilar didn't understand why her mother was trying to reassure her that she would be fine, when it was her mother who was sick, but then it suddenly occurred to Pilar that her mother had meant to tell her that she was dying. Pilar looked up, suddenly feeling overwhelmingly alone.

"You can't leave me," Pilar said, but only in a soft whisper. For some reason, she thought if she spoke her words any louder, it would be harder to bear.

"You have to believe me when I tell you that is the last thing I want," her mother responded calmly; too calmly. "But everything is going to be just fine for you. You're a strong girl, Pilar — a lot stronger than you know."

"This is a hospital," Pilar said. "They have to be able to make you better here."

"There are so many people in the world who love you, my sweet little girl. It isn't just me," Consuelo continued, not responding to Pilar's words or even acknowledging them.

"You mean Angel," Pilar said after a long silence had worked its way between them, realizing that there would be no negotiating what her mother had already planned.

"When I was growing up, Angel was always there for me. I could always count on him, no matter what."

"If you could always count on him, then why did you end up here?" Pilar asked, unconcerned for how insolent she came across; yet her mother seemed unaffected.

"I'm the only one responsible for what happened to me, Pilar. Angel tried so incredibly hard to help me, but I was too stubborn to let him."

"Even though you loved him?" Pilar asked, that having been obvious to her from the moment she first saw Consuelo look at him — that her mother had loved him once and possibly still did.

Consuelo paused for a moment before responding. "Maybe it was because of it — because I was too proud to let him know that."

Pilar was surprised by the honesty of her mother's response to her, coming across far more peaceful and confident than Pilar had ever known Consuelo to have been before, as if the knowledge of her dying had freed her somehow and enabled her to speak all the things that she'd never dared before.

"Don't be upset with Angel," Consuelo continued. "He's only trying to help."

"I'm not upset with him," Pilar replied, not interested in challenging her mother any more, knowing that there would be no point to that.

"Love will come to you in many different ways in your life. Be open to it, even when it doesn't indulge you."

Pilar looked at her mother curiously, uncertain exactly what she meant and far too tired to even try to pretend for her any more.

"Promise me that you won't ever settle for anything less than pure and absolute love, even if holding that love hurts you," her mother said. "Promise me," she insisted after another moment had passed without Pilar responding.

"Why?" Pilar asked.

"Because I need to be absolutely certain that you won't make the same mistakes I made in my life — I need to know that," Consuelo responded. "Promise me that, Pilar."

"I promise," Pilar said after a moment of hesitation; Pilar knew that when she spoke those words she would be releasing her mother from all that was left to tie her to the earth, and yet she also knew that her mother needed for her to say them.

Pilar laid her head against her mother's shoulder, knowing that her mother would caress her face and her hair, and needing that. Pilar allowed herself to simply enjoy the moment as it was, without concern for what would come to pass, accepting that there would be no more words between them.

That night her mother died, in her sleep and alone, much the way she'd lived her life — at least the part that Pilar had seen. Her mother had lived just long enough to make sure that everything that remained would be as she wanted, making both Pilar and Angel speak their promises to her. In her dying Consuelo was finally able to see her will absolutely done, if only for that one moment in her life.

25.

"What is that?" he asked.

"It's a map of the world," Pilar answered, moving the book closer to him. "This is where I'm from," she continued, pointing to Winnipeg on the map — at least, to the location where she knew it was, because it wasn't specifically labelled.

"But that's on the other side of the world," Jaime said, looking up at Pilar in disbelief.

"Yes, it is," Pilar responded, nodding her head to assure him that was indeed where she was from.

Jaime was a small boy, perhaps eleven or twelve years old, Pilar gauged. They had picked him up shortly after they arrived in Santiago, as they were heading out to her grandmother's house.

"Who's Jaime?" Pilar asked Carlos, the driver of their car, earlier in the day, after Angel had gotten out and walked over to a house; she had overheard Carlos and Angel talk about needing to pick up Jaime when they were at the airport, but hadn't dared ask Angel about him.

"Jaime is his son," Carlos told her.

"He has a son?" Pilar asked, more out of surprise than as an actual question.

"The senator is a very private man," Carlos commented, seeming to understand why Pilar would have been surprised by the revelation. "It's probably better for him that way," Carlos added after a moment.

It was morning when Pilar and Angel arrived in Santiago, having flown all night to get there. Even though Angel had gotten them the most comfortable seats at the front of the plane, Pilar had found it very difficult to sleep for any stretch at a time with all the commotion around her. Every now and then, she would catch people on the plane stealing glances at her and Angel and she had assumed it was because of her brace, but when they finally got off the plane Pilar soon realized that the stares they'd received had nothing to do with her at all — they were because of Angel.

"Senator Torres!" a woman called out to Angel the second they walked through the doors to the waiting area, startling Pilar; Pilar noticed a microphone in the woman's hand and a man with a video camera following after her, and she realized the woman was a reporter.

"Can you respond to the allegations that your sudden trip to Canada was to visit Consuelo Hernandez, who is alleged to have been involved with you and your ex-wife in the incident that saw at least four soldiers assassinated shortly after the coup?"

Angel quickly took hold of Pilar's hand as the reporter moved in closer to them, and Pilar was surprise by this — his motion had been quick and without hesitation, and was clearly meant to reassure her that she was safe with him.

"Why does the Ross family continue to prevent an investigation into those accusations?" the woman continued.

"Just ignore her," Angel instructed Pilar quietly as he led her out further into the waiting area, not bothering to respond to the reporter's questions.

"Senator — what about the claims that have recently surfaced that you were involved in the suspicious death of Felix Rodriguez? You've repeatedly declined to comment about the new eye-witness account that puts you in the area at the time of the alleged accident," the reporter continued as she followed them. "The first officer on the scene was your own uncle, after all — do you still have no comment about that?"

"My uncle's partner was Felix's own father — both of them arrived at the scene of Felix's car accident at the same time," Angel abruptly replied, clearly frustrated. "The real story that nobody seems interested in reporting about Felix Rodriguez's death is that his own father declared it an accident. And as for the soldiers — don't you think I'd be in jail or dead already if I really did have something to do with that? The reason the Ross family keeps preventing an investigation into the death of Colonel Ross and the other soldiers is because they know for a fact that I had nothing to do with it."

"The Ross family has consistently refused to comment on the matter," the woman continued. "Your father worked at the Ross family ranch for decades and there are rumours that he's had some influence."

"A poor peasant farmer influencing one of the richest and most powerful families in Chile — ? That's likely," Angel commented in turn.

Just then, Pilar noticed Angel look at a man who had walked up behind the reporter, but who had kept himself at a bit of a distance; Angel's look alone seemed to have spoken something to the man.

"The senator has important private matters he needs to tend to," the man said loudly, stepping in front of the reporter. "Please, save the rest of your questions for a more appropriate time."

The man escorted Pilar and Angel out of the airport and to a waiting car, handing Angel some papers along the way. Pilar watched Angel quickly flip through the papers as they walked along, disregarding the reporter and cameraman who continued to follow them and unaffected by the growing commotion as a group of curious on lookers started to amass. Either this was all perfectly normal for Angel or he simply did not care. Possibly, it could have been both, Pilar thought to herself after a while.

"My name is Carlos," the man introduced himself to Pilar after they all got into the waiting car, Carlos himself having taken the driver's seat.

Pilar could see Carlos' face only through the front mirror and noticed his eyes suddenly shift from her in the back seat to Angel beside him; Pilar could hear Angel speaking to him, but she couldn't quite make out his words.

"It's all being taken care of right at this very moment. Everything will be shipped by train with the police escort *Don* Rodriguez arranged," Pilar heard Carlos respond to Angel — his tone was quiet, but she was still able to hear him. "Did you want to pick up Jaime now?" Carlos asked, to which Angel nodded in response before continuing to look through the papers.

"Why do you speak Spanish like that?" Jaime asked Pilar shortly after Angel had introduced them, making Pilar feel suddenly self-conscious.

"She speaks it that way because it's not her first language," Angel quickly interrupted from his seat in the front; though he hadn't given Pilar even a moment to respond, she was grateful that he'd cut in. "Whenever somebody speaks more than one language, they always have an accent from their first language. For Spanish being her second language, I think she speaks it far better than you speak English, wouldn't you agree?"

"You speak English?" Jaime asked Pilar after a brief moment, this time speaking far more quietly than before, seeming to want to make sure Angel wouldn't overhear.

Pilar only nodded in response; nobody had ever told her before that she spoke Spanish with an English accent, neither Consuelo nor Pedro, and this assessment now left her hesitant to say anything more than necessary.

"Where did you learn that?" Jaime continued, appearing genuinely excited at the idea that she could speak English and making Pilar a little more at ease with that.

"In Canada, where I was born," Pilar responded.

"Canada? Where's that?"

That was when Pilar pulled out the map Pedro had given her just before she'd boarded the plane, the same one he'd shown her at the hospital the day Angel had arrived.

"This way you'll be able to see where you are and where you're going," Pedro had told her when he gave it to her, pointing out both Winnipeg and Santiago on one of the maps. "See — they're not so far away," he'd continued, leaving Pilar with the impression that he was trying to convince himself more than her.

Pilar and Angel had left Winnipeg for Chile just three days after her mother had died. She had barely had time to absorb the reality of her mother's death, let alone think of anything else, when Pedro came by with two small suitcases for her to pack her things in.

"Angel tells me you have quite a large family waiting for you back home," Pedro told her as he set down the suitcases in the living room.

"I guess," Pilar responded, knowing it would be rude for her not to say anything back but also finding it odd that he would refer to a place she'd never been to as her home.

"Just think of the adventure you have ahead of you," Pedro continued, clearly intending to help make her feel better but instead leaving Pilar feeling even more alone because she knew that whatever lay in store for her would be without any of the people she had known and loved in her life.

She opened up the suitcases in her bedroom later that evening, after having stared at them for the longest time. She looked at everything around her in her small room, finding it hard to absorb that she would be leaving the one place where she'd lived her whole life, likely never to come back again. She'd always felt herself to be drowning in that apartment, the sea of her mother's sadness having drenched everything that surrounded her, but now there was only dryness and emptiness, and without anything for Pilar to find her footing. It was only then that Pilar was finally able to cry — crying until her eyes burnt and she was physically incapable of crying any more. And then, after she had finished crying, Pilar started to pack her things, knowing that nothing in the world had changed with her grief — the earth had not shaken and time had not stopped.

The next morning, Angel and Pedro waited for Pilar at the front door.

"What about my mother's things?" Pilar asked, stopping to look in her mother's bedroom.

"I sent most of her things back to Chile already," Angel told her.

"To where?"

"To your grandmother's house," Angel replied. "Everything should have arrived by the time we get there."

"That's where we're going?" Pilar asked.

"For a while," Angel said, nodding his head.

"What about everything else that's left here?" Pilar asked, looking at all the furniture in the apartment.

"Pedro will help take care of all this," Angel responded.

Pilar looked at Pedro, and he smiled and nodded his head to reassure her.

Until that morning, Pilar had thought only about her own sadness, but it occurred to her then that Pedro's life was also changing beyond anything that he could control. Pilar knew that he hadn't needed to stay in that apartment block after finishing his university studies and getting a job as a high school history teacher, but he did it to help Pilar and her mother. For all those years, he had been there to support her, helping her with her homework and buying her paints and coloured pencils so that she could continue drawing when her mother could not afford to buy those things with the two small cheques she received each month.

"The one thing I know that you won't miss about Winnipeg is how cold it gets here," Pedro told her as they stepped out into the snow. "Now, you'll never have to feel this cold ever again."

Pilar couldn't look at Pedro directly then, knowing that she would cry if she did and that that would make Pedro feel even worse. Although Pedro was careful to hide his feelings from her, Pilar knew that he must have been just as sad as she was.

The ride to the airport that morning was long and quiet. Unlike their ride from the airport the day they'd picked up Angel, Pilar was grateful to be sitting in the back seat behind Pedro and Angel and that she didn't need to participate in any of the conversation. Pilar found comfort in being separate and alone then, and in not having to talk about anything. Instead, she took in the scenery as it passed by her — the greyed snow that covered everything and the small, dull-coloured stores and buildings. Even the sky was grey that morning, barely letting any light through at all.

When they reached the security gate area after checking in their bags, Pilar knew that she would have to say good-bye to Pedro, but she did not know how. Before she had the chance to even begin thinking of what she could possibly say to him, he pulled out the book full of all the world maps and gave it to her — stopping to show her where she was and where she was going.

"See — they're not so far away," he tried to show her.

"Aren't you going to thank Pedro, Pilar?" Angel suddenly interrupted the moment between the two of them.

Pilar was shocked by Angel's intrusiveness, by the way in which he tried to make her feel as though she'd done something wrong and by how he wanted to force her to speak when she was simply unable.

"It's okay," Pedro responded immediately to Angel's words. "Pilar can be shy sometimes," he clarified.

After some awkward glances between all three of them, Pedro spoke to Pilar again. "Take care of yourself," he said.

Pilar was unprepared for the softness of Pedro's tone and the way in which his words lingered thick between them, the sudden heaviness she felt in that moment stopping her from responding in the way she wished she'd been able to — to hug Pedro and tell him good-bye, and that she loved him. Instead, she disappointed herself in being able to offer him no more than a small smile of acknowledgement.

She glanced back at Pedro again just before she stepped through the doors to the security zone, curious if he was still watching her. He waved instantly and Pilar managed to find the quickness that time to wave back at him before the sliding doors closed behind her, separating her completely from him. In the car now as they made their way out of Santiago on their way to her grandmother's house, Pilar found herself replaying that small and simple moment in her mind, thankful for the certainty she felt that Pedro had understood.

"Why were you born there and not here in Chile?" Jaime asked Pilar, after studying the map for a moment.

"That's what the military regime did to this country," Angel answered from the front seat. "They divided families and pitted neighbour against neighbour. Some of those they rounded up and tortured managed to escape to other countries for safer lives — that's what happened to Pilar's mother."

Pilar stared at Angel, surprised by his explanation of how everything had come to pass, her mother never having explained it to her like that.

"Is it different now?" Pilar asked after a moment, Angel's words having suddenly made her feel uneasy about being there.

"Here? I think so," Jaime answered.

"Not much," Angel cut in again loudly from the front, without looking back.

Just then, Pilar noticed Jaime look down at her leg for a moment, then glance up at Angel. If Jaime had been curious about her brace, it seemed to Pilar that his fear of how Angel would respond if he articulated that curiosity outweighed anything else in his mind, and so he simply kept quiet. Oddly, sensing that made Pilar feel appreciative of Angel's presence — she could explain it to Jaime some other time, when she didn't feel so overwhelmed and tired.

Jaime fell asleep just after they got onto the highway outside of the city, after a silence had grown over everybody in the car. Pilar had been left disturbed by the way in which Angel had explained her mother's arrival in Canada and she was unable to think of anything else. Nobody had ever explained it to her that way before, not even Pedro. She wanted to ask Angel more, but didn't dare to — not only because she was uncertain how he would respond to her question, but perhaps more so because she didn't know if she was even ready to know more. Instead, she decided not to break the silence that had settled around them.

As they drove down the highway, Pilar watched the scenery. The highway was old and broken, with people walking along the side of it even when they seemed to be miles away from any house or town. Every now and then they would pass people riding horses or horse-drawn carts, and the modernness of the car they were in seemed oddly out of place alongside them. All the towns they drove through were filled with run-down and dusty houses, different from the houses she'd seen even in Santiago, let alone those back in Canada, and seeing them made her curious about the place from where her mother had come. Even the landscape around them was so different from what Pilar was used to; she hadn't realized just how flat Winnipeg was until they were about to land in Santiago, after seeing the Andes mountains peek out from the clouds just underneath the plane. Along the highway where they drove now, the mountains were more spread out, turning into smaller rolling hills, but the giant snow-filled peaks were still visible in the distance no matter how far they drove. Even the colour of the earth was different there, with its dense redness rising up into the air like a cloud whenever it was disturbed.

There in the car, with Jaime sleeping beside her and Angel and Carlos silent in the front, Pilar pulled out the fossil from her pocket — the one that Simon had given her all those years ago and which she'd kept in the night table beside her bed until the day she left. She needed to hold it in her hand, needing to be sure it was real.

26.

Pilar found it difficult to take her eyes off the two women — they seemed to be identical in every way that she could tell and that made her incredibly curious about them. Angel had led her down the church aisle that morning to the row at the front where her grandmother was already seated, and those two women were seated at the other side of Maria Soledad.

"These are my sisters, Maria Lucinda and Maria Mercedes," her grandmother introduced them to Pilar. "They're twins," she added after a brief moment, understanding clearly the question Pilar had in her mind without her even having to ask it.

When she saw them in the church, Pilar knew that the women were the same ones she'd seen the night before, in the car that took her grandmother from her house and into the darkness of the streets. Pilar had wondered if she was still groggy from sleep when she first saw them, because it seemed to her at first that it was the same woman but in two different places; it was only after she'd watched them for a moment longer that she realized they had to be twins.

When she had first stepped into her grandmother's house the day before, Pilar was immediately enveloped by the strong smell of mothballs. The smell stuck so thickly to the air that it seemed to her as if her grandmother had wanted to preserve everything around her and not just stop the moths from getting at the clothes.

"*Tía* Maria!" Angel called out after opening the door with his own key — and a moment later her grandmother appeared from around the corner.

Pilar hadn't expected her grandmother to look the way she did; that she was small and withered and old was not what she found unexpected about her, but rather that she was able to move around quickly and easily, seeming far younger in her step than Consuelo ever had.

"Finally, I get to meet my granddaughter," Maria Soledad said with a huge smile, moving in to give Pilar a hug; Maria Soledad then looked up at Angel. "You are going to stay here, aren't you?"

"Carlos is just bringing our bags in," Angel responded attentively, nodding.

"And Jaime?" Maria Soledad asked.

"He's helping Carlos."

"You must be tired from your trip," Maria Soledad said to Pilar. "Let me show you to your room so that you can nap a bit before supper."

Pilar looked back at Angel, awkward in her surroundings.

"I'll take your bags in later for you," he responded to her look.

As Maria Soledad led her to the bedroom, Pilar was surprised to find the house to be nothing at all like the first impression it gave her. The house was set directly against the sidewalk at the street and had no front yard at all, but when she walked deeper into the house, she found the entry hall led into a side corridor lined with windows facing out to the back, revealing a huge tiled patio with a lush fruit garden, a large shed and another yard behind that.

"Did my mother grow up in this house?" Pilar asked, surprised by how different it was from their apartment.

"Yes, she did," Maria Soledad responded. "Was your house in Canada similar?" she asked in turn.

"No," Pilar said. "But it was still beautiful," she added, thinking it to be the right thing to say to her mother's mother; in her mind, it was not a lie.

It was dark when Pilar woke up from her nap and she was uncertain how long she'd been asleep. She heard some faint noises coming from down the hallway, followed by the sound of the front door opening and closing, and so she decided to look out the window to see what was happening. Pilar saw a pick-up truck idling out on the street right in front of the house, its load covered tightly with a tarpaulin, and behind it was a black car. Angel stood at the far side of the pick-up and was talking to the man in the driver's seat. After a moment, he pulled out his wallet and gave the man some money. The truck then drove off, leaving Angel to watch as it disappeared down the road. After it was completely out of sight, Angel turned and walked over to the car behind him — the twins were in the front, and her grandmother sat behind them in the back seat. Angel spoke to the women briefly and then they, too, drove off, in the same direction as the pick-up truck had gone.

Pilar looked at Angel as he was left out in the darkness alone — he still looked in the direction the two vehicles had gone, even though neither of them was visible any more. It was the heaviness of his look and the length of time that he just stood there that told her the pick-up truck carried the coffins of her mother and her sister. Pilar had overheard

Pedro and Angel talk about Angela the day before they'd left Winnipeg, and even though she hadn't been able to make out all their words, she was certain that her mother would have wanted Angela to be taken back with them to Chile, and that wherever her mother's coffin was right now, Angela's was sure to be right beside it.

After another moment, Angel walked into the house and the street was left empty without him.

"Supper will be in about half an hour," Angel said after having knocked lightly on Pilar's open door just a few moments later. "I have your suitcases here — did you want me to bring them into your room?"

Pilar nodded at him and then watched him bring in her two small suitcases and place them at the foot of her bed.

"Your mother's funeral will be tomorrow morning," he said after a moment, looking directly at Pilar as he spoke; Pilar hadn't expected that he would and she immediately glanced away from him.

A brief silence filled the room, and then Angel quietly left. Pilar wasn't certain that she wanted him to leave, but it was all she felt capable of bearing in that moment.

The silence continued through supper and the next day through breakfast; Jaime was just as quiet as his father, perhaps scared to say anything when no one else was, and her grandmother was conspicuously absent. It was only later at the church, at her mother's funeral, that Pilar saw Maria Soledad again.

"Come sit by me here," Maria Soledad told her, motioning to a spot between her and her twin sisters.

Pilar felt odd sitting beside her grandmother's twin sisters when her own twin sister was in a tiny coffin in front of her. Consuelo had always told Pilar that Angela had accompanied her as she'd grown inside Consuelo's body, staying with her right until the day she was born into the world and not one moment less — she'd left Pilar's side only then, when she knew she was safely in her mother's hands. Consuelo had always told her that she knew Pilar would grow up to be a strong girl from that very first day, and that was why she'd given her such a strong name; Angela, on the other hand, was like the air and had needed to be freed.

Sitting in that room full of people who were largely strangers, on the other side of the world from where she knew home to be, Pilar wondered if in her dying Angela had meant to prepare Pilar for all the loneliness she would have to live through. Perhaps that was what her mother had sensed all those years ago.

A breeze welled into her room as she sat on her bed working on some drawings. It was evening and Pilar sensed that all the funeral guests had likely left, so she allowed herself to follow the breeze back to its source, knowing it was unlikely that she would have to talk again to people she didn't know. Earlier that afternoon, her grandmother's house had filled up with people wanting to offer their condolences and some had ventured to give Pilar a few kind words. Pilar knew that those people only intended to be supportive, but they were strangers to her and could not possibly have understood.

"It's a terrible thing for a mother to lose her child, *Señora* Maria," Pilar had overheard an older woman say to her grandmother.

Maria Soledad had sat in the parlour beside Angel all afternoon, at least for as long as Pilar had stayed there before heading off to her bedroom, needing to leave. It had been clear to her that the gathering was for everybody else except her or her grandmother, or even Angel, and so she'd gone to her room to wait until everybody eventually left.

Pilar followed the breeze now as it led through the corridor and out the open door to the back patio. Her grandmother was sitting outside on a chair with her eyes closed, seeming to be thinking deeply about something.

"Grandmother?" Pilar called out quietly, not wanting to startle her.

Maria Soledad opened her eyes slowly then.

"Why don't you bring over a chair from the shed and have a seat beside me?" her grandmother said after a moment of silence, and Pilar did just what Maria Soledad had instructed.

Maria Soledad had closed her eyes again by the time Pilar returned from the shed with a chair.

"What was she like when she was younger?" Pilar asked.

"She was very beautiful and she was the apple of her father's eye," her grandmother responded without opening her eyes. "Can you hear that?" Maria Soledad asked after a brief moment of silence.

"What are you listening to?" Pilar asked, not having heard anything in particular.

"Try to hear it," Maria Soledad responded softly, still not opening her eyes, motioning for Pilar to be quiet.

And so, Pilar sat quietly trying to make out what it was her grandmother was listening to — all she could hear, though, was the sound of cars driving by on the street every now and then.

Pilar wanted to ask her grandmother what it was specifically that she was listening to, but when she looked at her again, Maria Soledad still had her eyes closed and looked so peaceful, and Pilar did not want to disturb her grandmother. Instead, Pilar followed her grandmother's lead and closed her eyes, too, to focus her hearing better. Pilar let her mind's eye follow the sound of the wind as it moved through the leaves in the trees above her and out onto the street and beyond. It was almost rhythmic, then, the deep sound that suddenly came up underneath, and from the very moment Pilar distinguished it from the other sounds around them, she knew that it was what her grandmother was listening to.

"What is that?" Pilar asked, not daring to open her eyes as she did, for fear of losing the sound.

"It's the ocean," she heard her grandmother respond.

"The ocean? I didn't know it was so close," Pilar said, opening her eyes to look at her grandmother.

"Everything here is close to the ocean," Maria Soledad replied.

"I've never seen it before," Pilar told her.

"Then tomorrow I can ask Jaime to show you the way."

There was more silence between them after that exchange. Pilar studied her grandmother: how small and weathered she was; the wrinkles chiselled along her face and hands reminding Pilar of Pedro's scars; and her grey hair, with whispers of black laced between them, giving hints of what it had looked like when she was younger. Pilar couldn't even begin to imagine how old her grandmother was; she seemed so much older than Consuelo in many ways, and yet far younger in others. Maria Soledad had a lighter air than her mother had ever had, and the calmness that surrounded her put Pilar at ease.

"Who is Felix Rodriguez?" Pilar suddenly asked, sensing it would be safe to ask her grandmother that, having wondered about him ever since the burial earlier in the day.

Maria Soledad opened her eyes suddenly and turned to look at Pilar.

Pilar had noticed Felix's grave that afternoon, after the burial had ended and the people had started to leave the cemetery. She'd remembered his name from the airport, when the reporter had asked Angel about him, and so she lingered a bit by his grave, curious that she'd found him there.

"Did your father know him?" Pilar had stopped Jaime to ask him, motioning to Felix's grave.

"The three of them went to school together," Jaime responded, nodding.

"The three of them — ?" Pilar asked curiously, not certain whom else he'd meant.

"Felix, Dad and your mother," he clarified.

Pilar looked back at the grave again, at the dates listed under Felix's name — *1955 to 1974* — and realized he was the exact same age as her mother. The date of his death also struck her though, because it was the year she was born.

"How did he die?" Pilar asked Jaime. "A reporter asked Angel about that at the airport when we arrived."

"The reporters always ask him about that whenever he's in Santiago," Jaime commented in a matter-of-fact tone, the question clearly having been no surprise to him. "Felix was found dead just outside of town. He crashed his car into a tree and it caught fire before anybody could get out to help him. They say he'd been drinking and that was the reason for the crash."

"So why would anybody think that your father was involved?" Pilar asked.

"My dad gets blamed for a lot of things," Jaime said, shrugging his shoulders. "A lot of people don't like that he was elected to the senate and they make things up about him, but clearly *Don* Juan himself doesn't think he had anything to do with Felix's death even though Felix was a collaborator."

"Who's *Don* Juan?"

"Felix's father," Jaime said. "That's him right there," he added, pointing to an older man walking with a cane farther off in front of them.

"That's *Don* Rodriguez?" Pilar said, more as a realization than a question to Jaime, remembering that Carlos had mentioned his name in the car when they were just outside the airport.

Jaime nodded in confirmation. "I think he was a police officer with your grandfather."

Pilar studied *Don* Juan as he walked off ahead of them, something about him drawing her to look at him longer, though she wasn't able to pinpoint exactly what. Juan stopped to talk to her grandmother when he reached the front gates and for one moment as he talked to Maria Soledad — one very brief moment — he glanced back at Pilar; he looked at her the same way Angel had when he'd first come up to her at the airport in Winnipeg, with a deep sense of recognition. It was not his look, though, that surprised Pilar most about him, but rather the colour of his eyes: Pilar had not seen one other person in that small town with blue eyes like hers until then.

"Felix was a collaborator?" Pilar quietly asked Jaime after a moment, after *Don* Juan had finally walked out of the cemetery and disappeared from her sight.

"He turned people in to the army for money, right up until the day that he died," Jaime said, nodding his head. "He turned in a lot of my dad's friends then, and not just our mothers," he added casually, as if that were something Pilar should already have known.

That was the moment when Pilar suddenly needed to know exactly who Felix Rodriguez was to her.

"My dear sweet girl," Maria Soledad responded to her question now outside on the patio. "Trust me when I tell you this — there are some things in life you truly are better off not knowing."

"But there is something to know," Pilar said, her grandmother's evasiveness having confirmed at least that.

"The only thing you need to know is that people make mistakes in their lives because they love unwisely. They love with their hearts and not their minds, and they let their emotions guide them to places where they know they shouldn't go; sometimes, they can't ever find their way back."

Pilar looked at her grandmother, curiously sensing that what she'd said was not only about Consuelo.

27.

Pilar woke with a start in the middle of the night, full of fear — from a nightmare she assumed, yet she couldn't recall it. The darkness she woke into disoriented her and added to her sense of unease, and so she turned on the small lamp beside her to lighten the space around her. She found it curious that everything was exactly where it had been before she'd fallen asleep that night, given that she felt certain something had changed.

Earlier in the night, just before she'd gone to bed, Pilar had stared deeply into her eyes in the bathroom mirror, looking straight at the clear blue that stared back at her. She remembered hearing her mother cry in her bedroom after the therapist had asked her if Pilar's father had had the same colour of eyes. Pilar had thought then that her mother's tears were from the sadness of losing the father of her daughter, but when she looked at herself in the mirror there in her grandmother's house, she understood that memory in an entirely different way, and it was all she could think of that night.

She lay in her bed for a while after waking, then finally pulled out her book of drawings from the side table drawer where she'd left it when she'd first arrived, right beside her fossil. When she'd packed her things in Winnipeg, her paintings and drawings were the first things she'd put in her suitcase. Perhaps it was for the same reason that her mother never threw out any of the letters from her own father, even when the idea of his dying seemed too much for her to bear — they were proof of the life that had existed once, even as the memories themselves had started to fade away. Now, though, the pictures did not provide Pilar with any sense of comfort, but instead served only to remind her how alone she was. Even the sheets of blue that she'd made to comfort her mother all those years ago were not able to soothe her now in turn. The blue contained so many things that were not visible to the eye but which she knew were there — not just her mother's sadness, but also Simon's sorrow and the sense of loneliness Pedro always carried wrapped around him. Pilar closed her eyes in that moment, feeling the overwhelming need to do that.

"Are you all right?" she heard Angel ask, and she opened her eyes to find him standing at her doorway. "You have your light on, I wasn't certain if you were asleep," he continued.

"I'm fine," she replied, though she didn't understand why he would have woken in the middle of the night to ask her that.

"Did the tremor frighten you?"

"The tremor — ?"

"There was a small earthquake a few minutes ago; I thought that was what woke you up," he explained.

"I didn't realize that had happened," Pilar said, sitting up in her bed. "I didn't realize that it could."

"It happens here quite a bit," he told her.

"I didn't feel it," Pilar said after another moment. "I think maybe I had a nightmare, but I can't remember."

"*Tía* Maria told me you want to go down to see the ocean," he finally said.

"Yes," Pilar replied. "*Abuela* said that Jaime could take me tomorrow."

"I'll let him know first thing in the morning," Angel said, nodding. "Good night," he continued and then started to step back into the hallway.

"*Tío?*" Pilar suddenly called out to him; perhaps it was her exhaustion that made her braver. She had become so tired of all the things that were always being left unsaid.

Pilar met Angel's look straight-on when he turned to look at her again, needing to see how he would react to her question: "Did you kill Felix Rodriguez?"

"No — he was already dead by the time I arrived," Angel replied calmly, his tone telling her that her grandmother hadn't just told him about Pilar wanting to see the ocean; all Angel had left unsaid in his response, though, was not lost on her.

"He was my father," Pilar said, knowing that already and needing him to know that she knew.

"Felix wasn't much of anything to anybody, least of all to you or your mother," Angel told her.

"And what were you?" Pilar asked in turn, needing to challenge the certainty of his words.

"I was as much as Consuelo ever let me be."

"What could you be to her when she was on the other side of the world without anybody but me?" Pilar asked, her words clearly accusing him.

"Manuel and I asked her to come back many times after we were certain it would be safe for her, but she always had an excuse."

"And that made you feel better — ?"

Angel glanced at the brace beside Pilar's bed briefly, then looked back up at Pilar again. She turned away from him, not wanting to receive any sympathy from him.

"Every one of us has to deal with difficulties, Pilar," she heard Angel say. "Consuelo dealt with hers in her own way."

Pilar looked back at Angel then, caught off guard by his words. "Are you trying to tell me that she deserved what happened to her?"

"That's not what I said," Angel quickly responded, clearly upset. "Look at Pedro — without a question he's suffered more than any of us can even begin to imagine and yet where would you and your mother have been without him? He lost so much, and yet he continues to wake up every day and live his life."

Pilar was surprised by Angel's response, not having realized that in a matter of days he had learned more about Pedro than Pilar had over years. The truth was that Pilar didn't have any idea what it was that Angel assumed that she knew about Pedro. She only knew what was outwardly visible about him — the scars on his face and the photographs on the shelves in his apartment. Pilar hadn't expected Pedro to tell a virtual stranger more about himself than he had told her; she felt betrayed at first, but then grew more disappointed in herself for her part in having let that happen.

"I know this might be hard to understand, but Consuelo always did exactly what she wanted to do," Angel continued after a long silence had fallen between them.

"She loved you," Pilar said. "I think that's the only thing I know for certain about her."

Angel gave Pilar a small smile and paused briefly in thought, and Pilar wondered if it was because he had nothing to say to her, or perhaps too much. Finally, he stepped back into the hallway and walked away.

"Did you bring that back with you from Canada?"

"I think your dad did. It was my mother's."

"Those butterflies look just like the ones around here. There's a field just outside of town that's filled with them in the summer."

When Pilar had stepped out of her bedroom earlier that morning, her grandmother waved her over to her own room. There were boxes all over her grandmother's bed, and when Maria Soledad pulled out a few things from one of them, Pilar recognized them as her mother's things.

"Consuelo didn't tell Angel what to do with her things, just that she trusted his judgement," her grandmother told her. "Do you have any idea what we should do with them?"

Pilar was unprepared for her grandmother's question, given how little she felt she knew about her mother and the life she had lived.

"Her father gave this to her on her sixteenth birthday," Maria Soledad said as she pulled out the necklace Pilar remembered seeing tucked away in Consuelo's bedroom. "You should have it; I know Manuel would have wanted you to have it."

Maria Soledad's hands shook lightly as she put the necklace on Pilar, and Pilar thought it was because of her age; certainly it could not have been from nervousness.

It was then that Pilar noticed the butterfly box on her grandmother's side table — its shape and edges caught her attention and she knew it was the same box she'd seen in her mother's bedroom even though she hadn't gotten the chance to look at it closely. Pilar must have looked at it more longingly than she'd realized, because Maria Soledad walked over to it and picked it up without Pilar saying a word.

"Angel and Manuel made this for Consuelo when she was in elementary school," her grandmother told her. "Consuelo must have taken very good care of it to make sure that the glass didn't break after all this time."

Her grandmother held it out for Pilar to take, but Pilar hesitated even though she did want it. She remembered the last time she'd seen the box was when she was rummaging through her mother's things, not knowing how sick her mother was or that she was already in the hospital. Pilar had felt so bad afterwards for having invaded her mother's privacy that she never entered her bedroom again, not even all those nights she was alone in the apartment before Angel had arrived.

"Consuelo made us all sad," Maria Soledad said after a brief moment, still holding out the case for Pilar to take; it seemed to Pilar that Maria Soledad had intended her words to provide her absolution, not knowing how her grandmother could have known that was what she needed.

"Go show Angel your necklace," her grandmother told her.

"*Abuela* wanted me to show you this," Pilar told Angel a few moments later when she found him having breakfast, motioning to her necklace.

"Consuelo's necklace," Angel said. "It looks very pretty on you."

"Why did she want me to show you this if you already know what it is?" she asked.

Angel hesitated for a moment, seeming to need to think about the question before responding. "I suppose because it's rare when you get a second chance in life."

Angel then looked at all the things Pilar had in her hands — her pencil case and notebook, and the butterfly case.

"Did you need some help with those things?" he asked.

"No," she replied. "I want to take them down to the ocean with me."

"Jaime's out back," Angel told her. "Just let him know that you want to go now."

Pilar had asked Jaime to help her carry her things as they walked down to the ocean a short while later, and that was when he'd asked about the butterfly box.

In the very moment when he was telling her about the field filled with butterflies, the ocean suddenly appeared before them. Pilar hadn't expected it to happen that way, without any notice — they had just turned a street corner, one like the others they'd passed by on their way through town that morning, but now the ocean was right there in front of them. Pilar wondered how it could have been so close to her the whole time she'd been at her grandmother's house and yet be completely out of her sight, especially when it was so immense.

Pilar and Jaime sat down quite a bit away from the water on the sand, where Jaime told her they would be safe from the waves. There, Pilar started drawing the ocean for Pedro, so that he could know that she'd finally seen it, and for Simon also, even though she knew it was more than just physical distance that separated them.

"I have some extra pencils and paper if you want," she offered Jaime when she noticed him watching her.

"My dad says you're an artist," he said, clearly more curious about that than in drawing himself.

"I wouldn't go so far as to call myself that," she replied. "I just like to draw."

"You're very good," he commented. "I think if you can draw that well, that makes you an artist."

Pilar smiled at Jaime, knowing that he'd meant his words as a compliment.

"Your parents are divorced?" she asked him after a moment, noticing he was still watching her drawing; she'd wondered about it after nobody had mentioned Jaime's mother except for Jaime himself, remembering that the reporter in the airport had mentioned Angel's ex-wife as well as Consuelo.

"Yeah," Jaime answered, but then said nothing more.

"Did they stop loving each other?" Pilar asked.

"No, I think they love each other still," Jaime said after thinking about it briefly. "Sometimes, I can hear my mother crying at night after he's stopped by for a visit."

Pilar looked at Jaime and took in his melancholy expression; she thought it best not to disturb him any more with her questions.

The sound of the ocean crashing up onto the shore seeped in between them, and Pilar watched the water for a while, taking in its relentless rhythm — it was constant and steady and soothing, and seemed to be urging her to go to it, and so she finally did so, finding no reason to resist it. She took off her shoes and walked to the shore with her new drawing in hand.

"I'd be careful if I were you," Jaime called out from behind her. "The water's very cold and the current is very strong — it doesn't look that way from here, but it is."

Pilar glanced back briefly at Jaime, but then stepped in regardless. When the water rushed up to engulf her feet up to her ankles, though, she recoiled from its frigidity and instinctively stepped back out.

"The water here comes up from the Antarctica," Jaime explained.

Pilar looked back down at the water as it continued pushing itself up onto the beach and then pulling away again. For some reason, she felt it was trying to coax her into it again. She took a small step forward, this time allowing the water to touch the tip of her toes, but nothing more. She then set her drawing down on the water in a moment when it started to rush away from her and she watched as the ocean bobbed it hesitantly. Pilar wasn't certain if the water would take the picture, oscillating between pushing it back to shore and taking it out deeper — finally, though, she saw the picture gradually moving out farther and farther, and she knew that the ocean had accepted it. After another moment, a large wave rolled in and submerged the picture completely, and Pilar did not see it come up again.

"Weren't you happy with the drawing?" Jaime asked when she walked back over to him.

Pilar shrugged her shoulders in response, not knowing how to begin to explain it to him.

"Can you help me with my shoes," she asked him then. "My leg hurts and I don't think I can bend back down again."

"Sure," he said, holding out her shoes for her to step into; Jaime stared at her brace then, still obviously curious about it, but not saying anything even though Angel was not there to overhear.

"I have cerebral palsy," Pilar told him, seeing no reason not to tell him what he so clearly wanted to know.

"Does it hurt?" he asked.

"Sometimes the brace hurts me, especially if my muscles are tired," she answered. "But I wouldn't be able to move by myself without it."

"Did you want to go back home now?" Jaime asked.

"Yes," Pilar said, after briefly looking out at the ocean behind her again.

Some day, she would meld with the water and become part of it. She would be able to connect with everybody she'd ever loved all at once and no longer be separated from them by time or distance; she would be able to touch all the shores of the world and become both the rain and the snow. Until that day came to pass, though, all she could do was hold out her love and let it be carried.

CPSIA information can be obtained at www.ICGtesting.com
Printed in the USA
LVOW062107170113

316174LV00001B/2/P